"Each one of us has a spark within us, a spark made up of everything we are created to be. However, because of setbacks, distractions, and chasing after objectives others think are important, that spark grows dim and further away. Orlando Diaz, through a series of genre-bending short stories, explores the journey of a man rediscovering his spark—the beauty of his personal story in an empty, chaotic world."

—Daniel Hochhalter, Author—*Losers Like Us*

"Hands-down the most unique and clever book I've read all year, *Rosario Davez* enchants as much through the creative way it was written as it does through the adventures of its flawed and charming hero. Brimming with music, sass, love, and magic, this collection of stories will keep readers entertained and curious, all while challenging them to reflect on the insecurities we all face."

—Gina Dicarlo, Author—*The Western Passage* series

ROSARIO DAVEZ
SHORT STORIES

ROSARIO DAVEZ
SHORT STORIES

ORLANDO DIAZ

STORIES

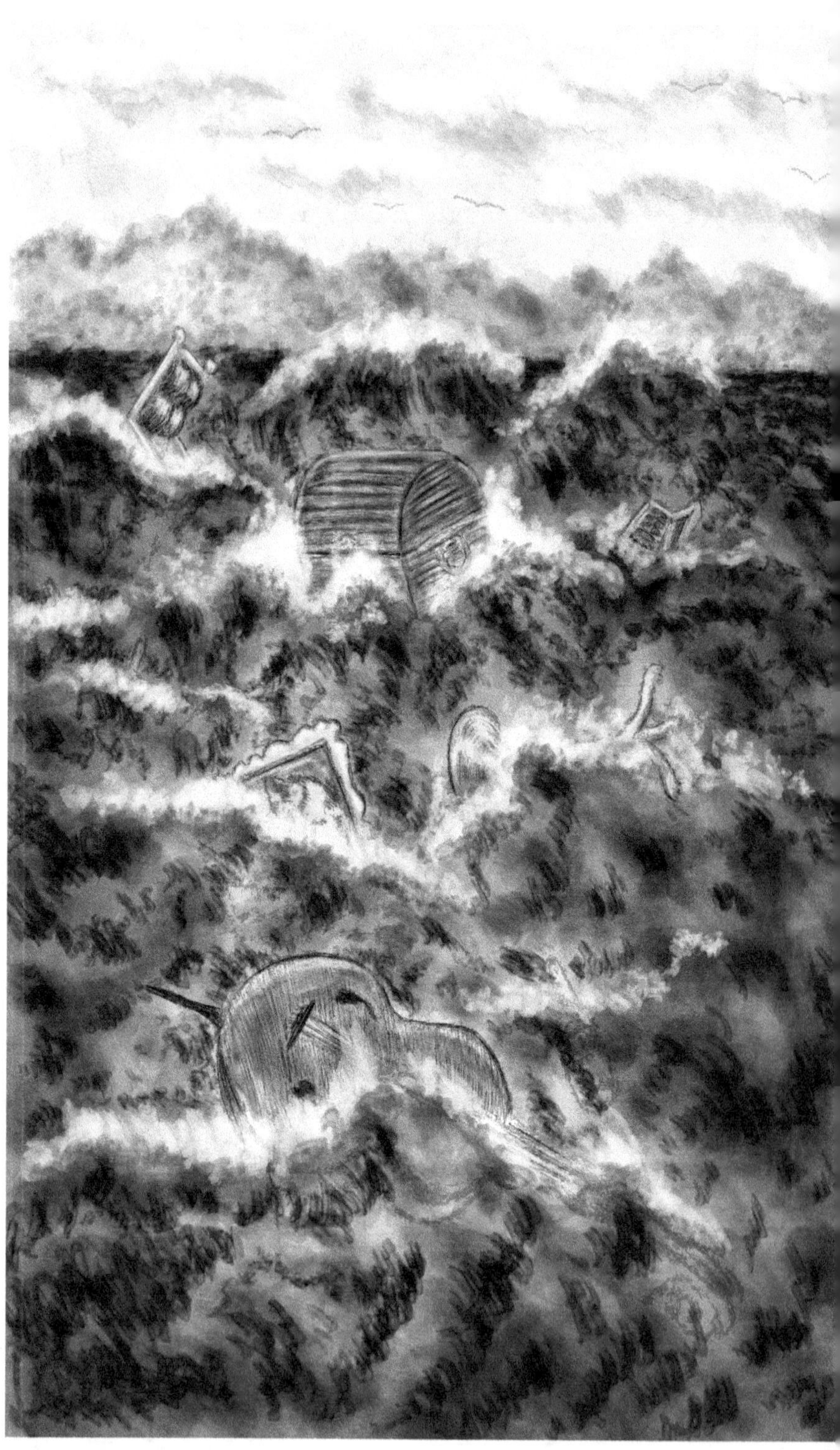

TWO BRAZILIAN MEN

There once was a profoundly rich man.
He had a lot of pride, he owned a lot of land,
He threw many large parties, and he played in many bands.
He was handsome, but try as he might,
he was a lonely, lonely man.

There was another man, an average poor man.
He owned next to nothing, lived near the sand
of the beaches where the waters feed into the Rio Grande.
He had a droopy eye, and he too was a lonely, lonely man.

Then one day, there was a flood at the house of the rich man.
His belongings floated down the river to
the beach near the Lagoa Mirim.
The poor man praised the Lord for the blessings he saw,
knowing whence they came, having seen the
man in his boats many times before.
But what did he do? What could he do to pass
the test with all the things of the rich man?

He swam out and retrieved all the things,
dried out what was salvageable and began
to fix anything that was damaged.
Within a week, the poor man, skilled in the art of
restoration, looked at everything and saw it was ready,
nicer than it had been when it was new.

Finally, the poor man built a raft to take
the rich man's belongings back.
He dragged the raft up the Pelotas, where
he found the rich man at his home.
The plan was to return everything lost and make a gift of the raft.
To his disappointment, he found the rich man busy,
ushering in a parade of replacement things.
Not wanting to interrupt or cause a scene, the poor man tied
the raft to a dock and began his journey north to São Gonçalo.

He was at the *lagoa's* first eastern turn when
he heard a shout from behind:
"My friend! My friend! ¡*Espérame*! Wait a minute!"
He smiled and turned around.

"*Amigo*, I cannot believe my eyes," said the
rich man. "Why did you do this?
I must give you something for your kindness;
you would offend me not to accept.
Please, come with me and I will pay you back handsomely."

But the poor man continued smiling.
"You have already given me the greatest treasure, rich man.
You see, years ago I was married to the love of my life.
We lived near the beaches of the Lagoa dos Patos.
She was the starlight of my days, the sunshine of my nights.
But, like your belongings, she too was taken
from me by the forces of the river.
For years, I have sat here along the banks in poverty,
praying for the Lord to return her to me.
If He truly raised Lazarus, I knew He could bring her back.
A long time passed, and I received no answer—
until I saw your treasures floating down the current.

"My love, you see, was a builder. A talented
woodworker and stonemason.
All her days were spent in the service of her
fellow man, building, fixing, and restoring.
So, rich man, you must understand it was her spirit
working with me that fixed your sculptures and clocks,
hammering your furniture and tables back into place.

"If you demand to bless me with objects and riches,
I only ask you not to give me your finest jewels, for
those are finished, good only for a viewing.
Give me your tattered and torn, that I
may play with my love again."

NOTICE!
NO DANCING
OREGON HIGHWAY ASSOC

FOUR DIAMONDS

Father

Brahman Davez was, like all creatures after the Fall, a broken man. He lived with his wife in a small apartment in Rio Piedras, Puerto Rico. Not many people would look at his life and say he succeeded at much, for he did not finish much that he started. All his life, it seemed there was always something standing in the way.

That something was of course, that ancient and deceitful serpent, laser focused on the destruction of the souls of men. The battle between Brahman and the serpent had raged for years, and like a championship chess match, it was anyone's game.

To his credit, Brahman possessed something no one else on the planet possessed: faith.

I do not speak of any traditional religions or even a singular belief in a person or ideology, so some may say this was not really a "faith" in any interpretation of the word.

Nevertheless, by the time he had achieved his adulthood goals of marriage, a job, and a house, Brahman believed in this faith so strongly that it could not fail, regardless of what that ancient serpent threw at him.

This faith was gifted to him after a concert of Rachmaninoff's Third Piano Concerto by the late, great Emil Gilels. He was emancipated by the way Gilels made notes pop out of nowhere like a sorcerer, the way his melodies surprised each other with an elegant humor.

On his way home from the concert, Brahman could think of nothing else. A decision was made that night. After a lifetime of musical appreciation, this concert was the baptism by fire for Brahman's faith. His new creed: a strong musical education in the Russian style of classical piano playing was humanity's most valuable asset.

Immediately, he contacted every one of his friends in search of musical wisdom for himself. Several of his school and work colleagues were amateur musicians. Some gave him pointers; others went as far as to give him lessons. For months this went on, his passion unceasing. Time and time again, however, he would hear a small voice in his head that kept whispering: *You are a bit too old to be starting this, don't you think?*

His wife, Martila, initially could not understand why he took to this idea so strongly. There was no convincing Brahman away from it, so to support them, she took on extra jobs while he practiced his new craft. Progress was slow and barely noticeable. But Brahman's faith was unshakeable as the mountains, even as that little voice in his head resounded every night, tempting him to quit.

A year into this, Brahman decided to put on a concert. A small showing, for his friends and family. On the program were a variety of small pieces by common practice composers—Clementi, Kabalevsky, Bach. The reception was sweet, and his teachers were proud. Not that anyone was counting, but he made forty dollars in donations. This was great because it covered the cost of post-recital refreshments.

"So, it wasn't a total waste of time," Martila said, smiling, in passing.

And so it happened that Brahman ran headlong into his first existential crisis. Was that all she had to say? His wife of five years? Some support! And his friends—was *anyone* moved? Did they hear *anything* special in his music? Brahman didn't really know what he was expecting, but by the end of the night, he knew he was miles away from whatever it was he was searching for.

But, as his wife was pregnant with their first son, Brahman decided it was best not to bring it up. Martila tended to get emotional about everything he said, so he treaded carefully around her.

"Yeah," he laughed. "I guess so long as we can get free cheesecake bites whenever we want, I think I'll quit my day job!"

Martila frowned. "Don't."

It took everything in Brahman's power not to slap his wife at that moment. He wished he didn't get so angry all the time, but this was inexplicably important to him. Nothing he said or did was able to translate this importance to Martila, who continually refused to verbally acknowledge her support for Brahman. (Of course, being the man he was, he also refused to acknowledge the way she unbegrudgingly worked hard to keep food on the table for the both of them.)

Eventually, Martila reached her third trimester. As headstrong as she was, she had to take time off work. It was a stalemate attempt at good husbanding that led to Brahman taking a job as a hardware technician.

After a while, his musical passion began to wither. His days were filled with machines and welding tools. He could hardly bear the silent judgment from his wife every time he brought up his passion or even practiced his scales and arpeggios. Though his radio was regularly tuned to the classical music station, his keyboard began to gather dust. He wondered why marriage had to be such a war, and if their son, due in just a week, would thrive in this environment.

He arrived at an idea, one he would fight for like nothing else in his entire life.

When he broke the news to his wife, Martila was frustrated but submissive.

"You're going to force him to be a *pianist?* He could be a doctor, a lawyer, a president, anything! What is this obsession with the piano?"

But Brahman was headstrong and stubborn. All he replied was, "It is decided."

Their son would become the great pianist Brahman was unable to be himself.

For five years after the birth, Brahman formulated a strategy to manifest this asset in his son. He traveled the nations seeking mentors and coaches, but it seemed every person he met was either an abysmal piano teacher, had their kids taking torturously bad piano lessons, or neither, making them functionally illiterate. These challenges he continually faced until one day, a friend of Brahman invited him and his wife to a witch's castle in Guaynabo for a party.

It was not far and they had nothing better to do, so the three of them made the journey.

Christa Nylssen was a massive woman with a magical touch. Her castle was protected by a community of battle-hardened social workers, and during the day she taught piano lessons to an entire island of tired Puerto Ricans. Every night, she hosted parties that lasted until daybreak.

From the great Russian tradition herself, Christa Nylssen had heard of Brahman and his search for a great musical education. That night, they were introduced.

"You have traveled far and faced many challenges and disappointments, Brahman. Yet this is the life you want for your son, correct?"

"Great witch, your castle is wondrous and your pupils gleam with a supernatural pride. Whatever the price, I will pay for my son to join their number."

"Sit down and let me tell you the treasure I seek. Then we can discuss payment."

At this, the lights in the hall dimmed. As if on cue, the rest of the partygoers sat down and turned their attention to the great witch Christa.

"You must understand, Brahman: though I live in this enchanted castle, it is cursed. Though the entire island pays for my extravagant existence with personal chefs and special varieties of mango, though I've been gifted with an unnaturally long life and air conditioning, and though inside the secret music boxes and big, big pianos lie an unlimited store of wine, I cannot walk very well, as you can undoubtedly see."

And Brahman did see. Her hips juggled a sort of balancing act to the point where every step she took performed a graceless Lindy Hop. Driving the point home, Christa took two steps forward, for all intents and purposes looking like a wounded deer.

She continued.

"In the dawn of time, four diamonds were buried in the earth, and each diamond carried a purpose to balance the planet:

"The *Diamond of the Step* gave its host the ability to traverse any terrain, material and immaterial.

"The *Diamond of the Breath* was a selfless catalyst, its host carrying the solemn duty to set captives free in body, soul, and spirit.

"The *Diamond of the Horn* strengthened the host to fulfil the deepest desires of their heart.

"The *Diamond of the Thorn* held the host to the gathering and reburying of the diamonds—through his or her own sacrifice.

"For generations, the Diamonds have remained hidden. They were last gathered somewhere in modern-day Palestine almost two thousand years ago. Rumors often spread of their discovery, and I made the journey to see for myself time and time again, but time and time again, it turned out only to be wild hallucinations of alchemists, driven mad by the search."

At this, Brahman stood and said, "They must still be in Palestine, then. Let us go and find them, so you can teach my son."

Christa shook her head lovingly. "After years of political and religious struggle, I doubt the Diamonds would choose to remain in such an area. Not very subtle."

He was confused by this, but before he could reply, the embarrassed Martila pulled him down and told him to be quiet.

"Yet your interpretation is right," said the witch. "I seek the Diamonds, even one. It was set in motion from the dawn of creation that whenever the four Diamonds are gathered and buried, they are destroyed. They must be born anew from the four corners of the earth, but their creation is a mystery, even to me. As far as anyone knows, they may choose to be born in the feces of a wild kangaroo or inside the forgotten soup bowl of a queen's palace!

"Yet I hold fast, knowing this to be true: one cannot force inspiration; one can only prepare the vessel. This is why I spend my days in the training of pianists in the great European musical traditions. I do my best to cultivate in my gleaming pupils the ability to bear a Diamond on my behalf."

Suddenly, the lights in the hall changed again. Music began to play, and the partygoers resumed their earlier conversation.

Brahman and Martila approached Christa.

"This is beyond anything I could have expected, great witch," said Brahman. "And yet I do not understand—why do you train the next generation to bear a treasure you yourself desire?"

Christa looked at Martila and laughed. "The audacity of the penis, no?" She turned to Brahman. "Is this not what you seek yourself, stupid man? A treasure for your son that you yourself are unable to reach?"

Though flushed with embarrassment, he could not help but smile at these two women. For the first time in a long time, he saw Martila smile as well.

"For years," said Martila, "I have seen my husband chase this fool's ideal. It is for the first time tonight I see a glimpse of the treasure. I thank you, Christa. It will be an honor to have our son raised by your great pedagogy."

The witch looked at them affirmingly. "When your boy is three days shy of his sixth birthday, bring him to me."

Son

So, three days before my sixth birthday, I began my journey into this piano world. My parents introduced me to the sorceress, and in spite of Christa's loveliness and desire that I lead a normal kid's life, the hours of practice my father required of me made it seem like I did not see the sun for about a year. Looking back at the momentousness of this event, it is a hilarious miracle how little I thought of the piano in my adolescence. The truth is, the first few lessons were sweet and focused primarily on physicality, my small hands interacting with such a massive instrument. It was a little boy and his *madrina* (godmother), huddled close and making sure little Rosario didn't overwork or hurt his precious hands. A true woman of magic, that Christa Nylssen.

(Did you know, dear reader, that by drilling the gentle treatment of the wrists at a young age, you can protect an entire lifetime of battling carpal tunnel and tendonitis? I tell you the truth, to this day, I have never had any pain in my hands. Not even once. This may not mean much to the average reader, but what if I told you that ninety-nine percent of musicians report pain caused by their instruments at some point in their life?)

That first year was a simple time. There was a small digital keyboard in the room where I slept. The keyboard also served as table for small magazines with girls I thought were pretty. I believe they belonged to my grandmother. My little self would practice the piano for a couple of minutes then spend some time kissing the pictures of these girls. I assumed they were the inspirations for Disney's *Pocahontas*, *The Little Mermaid*, et cetera.

Meanwhile, many strides were made in the piano lessons. These were foundational times for me, though I knew it not. Nowadays, my social feed is filled with lazy parents and pathetic children who talk about "playing by ear," as if that carried any merit: "I never learned to read music, but I can just hear music and play it on the piano."

This would never have passed with Christa Nylssen. In fact, one of the first things the great witch introduced me to was a skill that would eventually make me unstoppable—not that I realized it at six years old.

She called the skill *solfeggio*, the skill of proficiently reading music off a page, where it flows off the fingers as easily as these words of mine are flowing through your brain. Drill after drill, Christa Nylssen pounded into my head not just the written language of music, but a deep, intrinsic knowledge of notes and their relation to sound. Every day, she and my father developed in me that most valuable of assets: a strong musical education in the Russian style of classical piano playing.

Dear reader, for your sake and the sake of thy progeny: do not seek an easy path to greatness; you will fail and cause much destruction.

After a few years, I became exceptionally impressive at playing the piano. My weekly time with Christa was the highlight of my days, as she would show genuine interest in my life.

Also, I don't know how this is possible, but there was a point in our lessons where she was no longer an old woman.

It did not happen overnight. For the last several months, her castle had undergone a subtle change in color, as if someone were bringing out the yellows in contrast with the shadows. I suppose I was too small to notice such things at the time, but as her home brightened up, so did she.

I remember the day I really noticed it. One Saturday, my father dropped me off at Christa's castle for my lesson. I knocked on the door; no one answered. This was normal, as I could always hear the previous lesson going on, so I let myself in.

Her student was blazing through the middle section of Chopin's *Polonaise in A-flat*, the pinnacle of pianistic achievement in her school. I watched in amazement as the student's left hand effortlessly slid down the octaves in the E-major section.

Something in the performance was enlivening Christa as well, and for the first time, I realized the witch who had initially taken me in and the woman who sat there before me were vastly different people. While at the start of our lessons years ago, Christa was a loving, old woman with a limp, my piano teacher now was an inarguably younger version of the same person. While still old, she was slim and sexy, wearing a yellow tracksuit and her lush, brown hair up in traditional Ukrainian fashion.

Her wonderful, loving nature had not changed, however. Once my talent was ready for public spectacle, I had her to thank for the school and church functions that would hire my young and free talent for events. Those lucky dogs had me on a regular basis, and at each lesson, Christa would ask me how the gigs were going.

"In all honesty, the church gig last night was awkward. They put me in a tent and expected me to play for a group of people with nothing to do but listen to me."

"Oh, so it was a concert?"

"I guess so. But I didn't really have anything prepared, since I usually play background music. I played "The Girl from Ipanema" and then improvised for about ten minutes. Then, when I got up to leave, all of a sudden, I had this awful headache—still hurting me today."

"Aw, come here, little Rosario. Let's see if your *madrina* can't help you out here."

I was probably fifteen years old at this point, but I still become a little boy at Christa's castle. I snuggled up to the woman and she rubbed my head to make it feel better. It tickled, and I let out a big sneeze, knocking my head into the piano.

"Oh no!" she said, then noticed something in my ear. She pulled it out.

I freaked out for a second. "Oh, God. What is that?"

At this point, Christa's face grew serious. She stood up, walked over to the phone, dialed a number, and waited.

"Hello, Brahman."

I hear my father on the line. "Yes?"

Then she stands there silently. She looks over at me; I'm confused out of my mind. A moment passes.

"Hello? Everything all right?" he says.

"Uh, yes. Sorry, just wanted to let you know Rosario and I are going to take a little longer today. He's making great progress, your boy. Come by in an hour."

She hung up the phone and walked back. I noticed that she didn't have her usual limp, and I mentioned it.

"Hey! You're walking normally today! It's a miracle!"

Christa smiled and said quietly, "It's a funny bug. Keep it and everyone will think you're hilarious."

I was so confused. This was not like her at all. When I started to say something, she quickly went back into teacher mode.

"So, what are you going to play for me today?"

Christa was not one to keep information from me, but I was uneasy. Looking back, I understand why she didn't tell me right then and there that I was to be the host to the Diamond of the Step, though part of me wishes I had prodded more.

Interestingly enough, however, when I put the "funny bug" in my pocket and went back into lesson mode, I almost immediately forgot about it.

"It's the *Scherzo* today. Get ready to be blown away."

She wasn't.

Godmother

It was a little less than three years before this piano lesson with Rosario that I found a Diamond of my own.

The year was 2005, and there had been rumors circulating about a potential Diamond in a field of flowers in northwestern Oregon. Rumors like this were common, but as I was getting older and more desperate, I rarely let rumors slide. Plus, it was always an opportunity to travel with my beloved students. For this journey

I brought with me four of my most luminous pupils: Jaxon, Lyla, Mariali, and Brayden. These four lived in the castle with me, working and serving the community with much joy and singing. For the trip we carried nothing with us except our walking sticks. No bread, no bag, no money in our belts.

The journey from Puerto Rico to the Northwest was one I personally had made many times before. Oregon and Washington seemed to be popular spots for alchemists and diamond-seekers. *And why not?* I said to myself. *They are clean and green, their waters flowing from pure Olympian aqueducts.*

On the way, tavern keepers and old friends invited my crew and me to pass a night of merry music making. One of the tavern keepers asked if we were heading to the field of flowers where a Diamond was rumored to be in hiding. Smiling, I responded in the positive, hopeful that my reputation preceded me.

The tavern keeper laughed and asked, "And what if you find it? What then?"

"God only knows," I replied, "but I seek the day I see the curse lifted from my body, where I may sing the song of Simeon one last time:

> *Lord, now lettest thou thy servant depart*
> *in peace, according to thy word:*
> *For mine eyes have seen thy salvation,*
> *Which thou hast prepared before the face of all people,*
> *A light to lighten the Gentiles,*
> *And the glory of thy people Israel.*

After a tired round of applause, the tavern keeper smiled at me. I recognized that smile, having seen it on many a face who did not believe in Diamondlore. As the years had passed, I grew accustomed to seeing this smile, though it always made me sad. To many, the Diamonds were like an old religion. I could hardly argue with this, considering their last reported burying coinciding with the death and resurrection of Jesus Christ. But to me, the Diamonds represented something exciting, a change in humanity. Since I was a little girl, I have wanted more than anything to be near the Diamonds when they next were sent.

Alas, to most I was just a weary old lady. So as usually happens, travelers rested that night, singing of the great heroes. Every night we stopped at an inn; every night I told my story and sang my song. Nothing out of the ordinary until we reached Gresham City.

In the morning, we passed a fig tree in leaf. I was hungry and poked around to see if the tree had any fruit; it did not. Though Mariali and Brayden warned me of what this omen historically meant, I ignored them and traveled on.

The next day, we passed through a vineyard, grand and guarded by a wall, ten feet high all around. There was a large pit dug on the northern side of the vineyard for the winepress, and a watchtower on the southern side. The farmers granted us passage in exchange for small coinage, and as we went through, we picked some grapes for a snack. The vineyard was beautiful to behold and the grapes were sweet. To our horror, however, as we exited the vineyard, we saw two dead bodies outside the wall on either side of the road.

The corpse on the west side was an old man with a blue diamond ring the size of a tangerine. Lyla reached forward only to have me smack her upside the head. I pointed to the other corpse; it was a younger man. Both hands had been cut off. Again, Brayden warned me of the omen.

"Unnerving. Who would do this, and what kind of place harbors or allows this? And why would you lead us into those places?"

I was silent. In all the years they had studied with me, they had never caught me choked for words. Reading in this an insecurity, Mariali and Brayden made the decision to turn back. They reentered the vineyard while Jaxon, Lyla, and I continued.

It was late and the night was humid. We stopped to rest in the mouth of a cave overlooking the field of flowers where the Diamond was rumored to be hiding; we still had a day's journey to go. Lyla took the first watch while we slept.

As the night quietly rolled around, a man came into the other side of the cave to relieve himself. They made eye contact, she and he. Though slightly embarrassed, Lyla put a finger to her mouth, signaling the peeing man to keep quiet so as not to wake the others. The man nodded and turned around to finish his business.

As he did, another man, much younger, came out from deeper in the cave wielding a dagger, sneaking past our sleeping group. He looked straight ahead, not noticing us. The startled Lyla started toward him, but the young man put a finger to his lips. Not wanting to cause a scene, the pupil sat back down and played with some sticks, her bravery spent for the night.

The young man approached the peeing man and cut off a corner of his robe. He did this in one sweeping motion, so the peeing man was unaware and did not flinch. He finished his business and walked out of the cave. Clutching the clothing, the young man smiled at the cowardly pupil and ran back into the depths of the cave. A few min-utes later, Jaxon woke up and took over the second watch.

In the morning, we embarked from the cave, the field look-ing like thirty acres of daffodils. Upon reaching it, we discovered a mass of sticky figs all over the ground. With each step, our legs grew heavier under the weight of sticky figs accumulating under our shoes. So, we hatched a plan. Jaxon would take the first trek into the field, as far as his chubby legs would take him. When the weight became too much to bear, he would undress his feet to go as far as he could barefoot. Meanwhile, Lyla would carefully place her steps in the exact footsteps as Jaxon left, avoiding picking up unnecessary sticky figs. Lyla would bring Jaxon a clean pair of shoes, washed by my own hand.

It was a tedious process to be sure, but after a few hours of this, we found an already trodden path deep in the field, free of the sticky figs, and a man sleeping on the cleared floor. We woke him up.

"Ah, seek ye the Diamond as well?"

"You have seen it?" I asked, shocked to receive such a clear confirmation.

"Oh, yes. But like the others, you won't be pleased when you find it."

"How do you mean?"

"It is inside an orange flower, a stone's throw in that direction." He pointed north, and there indeed sat an orange daffodil.

At first glance, it was an almost unnoticeable shade of differ-ence from her bright yellow neighbors, but as we walked toward it, we realized it was orange. But it wasn't orange by design: it was orange by disease. The flower was sickly to be sure, and as our group leaned down to behold the Diamond, Jaxon, and Lyla were certainly disappointed.

Dear reader, I don't know if you have ever seen a rough, uncut diamond up close. Of course, it takes a lot of work and pressure to turn the stone into jewelry for pious American housewives. But no amount of processing would improve this Diamond, barely visible and dark, an impure form of crystalline diamond, graphite, and amorphous carbon.

The emotions running through my body at this moment could have powered a small country. There, in front of me, was the legendary Diamond of the Horn, created to "strengthen the host to fulfil the deepest desires of their heart."

But not everyone saw what I saw, for the world of commercial stone was a weakness for Lyla, and I realized too late the true reason she had come on the journey. Fancy black diamonds from nature are relatively profitable, obviously depending on the sought after size, but they will likely go for anything between three thousand and five thousand dollars per carat. To Lyla, however, this rock looked more like a legless stinkbug than a diamond.

She sat down and began scraping her shoes, a defeated frown weighing down her lovely face. I imagined this look on the many who had sought the Diamond, expecting something of physical beauty but finding instead a thing most anticlimactic. I saw Jaxon was disappointed as well. Of course, none of us had ever seen any of the original Diamonds of lore before, but surely, there had to be an overzealous hype about it all. A hokey religion, with its own prophecies and mad adherents.

Jaxon truly loved me like a mother. But this trip, its omens, and the final discovery of a worthless rock in a sickly flower . . . no more would he follow the witch. He turned to me and saw me weeping.

"Will you take it?"

I leaned ever closer to the flower and blew on it. A cloud of pollen lifted into the air. I responded quietly.

"What did you expect to find, young Jaxon? A reed swaying in the desert? A spectacle of refracting lights?"

He chuckled. "Honestly, I have no precedent. But this, Christa? This is embarrassing."

"Embarrassing?" I ask surprised, not lifting my gaze from the flower. "Because she is small and dark? *Nigra sum sed formosa.*" I let out a sniffle.

He adjusted his stance. "Will you now let your servants depart in peace, according to your word? For I have seen the Diamond, which has prepared you a light to be a light to end your days."

At this, I found myself becoming gratefully aware of his youth and innocence. Jaxon had always been my favorite; as much as he saw me as a mother, I viewed him as a son.

"You have always had the choice, young Jaxon. I cherished your company all these years and am so proud of the man you have become. As for me, I will take the stone and discover what it means for me and the world. I would be grateful for your company on the return journey, but feel no need to accompany further."

Thus, I took the Diamond and placed it in my pocket. The man lying down on the path chimed in, "Best not put her in your pocket. This one needs a little room to breathe."

With a cough, he lay down and fell into a deep sleep. He rolled over onto his side, revealing an entire backside encrusted in sticky figs. Then, as if his body was a balloon letting out air, his clothes sank to the ground and the man was no more to be seen.

On the journey back, Jaxon and I talked of his dreams upon our return. He planned to marry Lyla and move to the southside of the island. (Eventually, they did end up doing just that, though the marriage was short-lived due to her ambitious promiscuities. We kept in touch the whole time, with him seeking my advice constantly and listening infrequently.)

As for me, my first step on returning to the castle was to create an environment the Diamond could develop in. For months I took care of it, polishing it, serenading it with my student's music, playing with it like a child plays with a doll, dreaming of the day when it would do as prophesied and grant me my heart's desire.

Every day I spent with the Diamond gave me vibrancy and youth, so that many claimed I was reborn of demonic influences. I couldn't help but laugh at that.

The Diamond of the Horn famously keeps its owner in a youthful state and immerses the host in hope, though after my journey, it occurred to me how rare belief in Diamondlore had become. It made me sad to witness this loss of faith because it is often such a mundane process. When people cease to see miracles, it is not because they no longer believe they exist. It is because they no longer look for them.

Faith does not aim to be easy, of course. I realize now, as I write this, why I was not given what I thought was my heart's desire. But at the time, I could hardly contain my frustration. For such a long time I had been cursed with a limp, and try as I might, exercising all the faith I could muster, my Diamond could not and would not rid me of my malady. Instead, it seemed to draw *more* attention to it, for why would such a beautiful woman have such a bizarre gait?

So, imagine the conflict within me when this major inconvenience, this curse upon my body, briefly left me as I held in my hand the Diamond retrieved from the ear of young Rosario Davez.

I stood up and phoned his father.

"Hello, Brahman."

"Yes?"

I found myself standing there silent. I looked over at Rosario, his young, naïve face fixed in an eternal grin.

"Hello? Everything all right?"

I wanted to tell him; I really did. I wanted to tell him of my trip to Oregon and my discovery. I wanted to tell him how I had spent the last couple of years raising the Diamond of the Horn to power and how it had given me youth and beauty. Most importantly, I wanted to tell him that the Horn had succeeded in helping me find another Diamond, which turned up in his son's ear, of all places.

But I could not do it.

Brahman was a proud man, and his influence on his son would be devastating if he found out. I shall not go into it here, but over the years I had come to know Brahman and the family; I could no longer trust him. So cruel to that boy and his mother. No heart, no passion. Only money, always making wrong decisions, only visions of the dividends. If I told the father, he would likely find a way to extort the magic of the Diamond. If I told Rosario, the same would happen. He was much too young for me to ask him to keep a secret from his father.

Frozen, there I stood. I had always assumed my Diamond would one day lift the curse from my body, that I would walk normally again. But this would be a small victory compared to what I had built my pedagogical career on: to prepare a vessel for the bearing of a Diamond. I thought of the Horn in my room and shed a tear of gratitude. She had undoubtedly given me my true heart's desire.

I could not tell Brahman about his son. Brahman must never know his son was the host to the Diamond of the Step. And so, I could not be the one to tell Rosario, at least not any time soon. He was still too young and too close to his father. My only hope was that one day, when the time was right, one of the other Diamonds would meet him and they would proceed, unhindered in their holy duty, whatever that would be.

"Uh, yes. Sorry, just wanted to let you know Rosario and I are going to take a little longer today. He's making great progress, your boy. Come by in an hour."

I hung up the phone and walked back.

At the top of his lungs, Rosario shouted, "Hey! You're walking normally today! It's a miracle!"

I gave him back the Diamond of the Step and said, "It's a funny bug. Keep it and everyone will think you're hilarious."

We went back to the lesson and he played Chopin's *Scherzo No. 2.* I was not impressed.

Son (on the Subject of Girls)

Somewhere around twelve years old, the age at which Jesus Christ scared the ever-loving crap out of Mary and Joseph, was the age I realized an odd but life-changing truth.

Not everyone thought I was as cute as my mom thought I was.

Does this happen to everyone? Was it just the funny bug in my ear, or was there something else? At the time of this writing, I am single as a tumbleweed, though every once in a while there will be some intimate miscreancy I am not too proud of. Always I remain hopeful—recently took a girl out to get pedicures and Chic-fil-A. We'll see how that turns out.

Girl season for me started a few years later when I was sixteen. My family and I were living in Hillsboro, Oregon. It happened over the course of three nights which I will now recount. The tale is like a mixture of the Rhinemaidens of *Das Rhinegold* and the ghosts of *A Christmas Carol*.

Night One: Adalyn

The first was a bright-blue princess, who spent most of her life as a star. She addressed me as "little boy" and took me for a ride. Her name was Adalyn, her eyes piercing through all my observations. I was sleeping naked that night, and she taught me how ignorant I was to believe the things I did.

We spent the first part of that night seeing my favorite band, even though my finger was broken. The band was the Alan Parsons Project.

After the last song, "Breakdown," we talked for hours about people and dreams and hopes and whether the band really enjoyed what they did. Probably not. Music is the worst.

At the end of that night, I leaned in for my first kiss.

Whiplash.

"Little boy, that is not my job."

Thus, the night ended, and I chewed on cardboard all the next day. But the day was bright.

There's something about being visited by shiny blue princesses that stays with you. I treated my family differently. All of a sudden, I had caught a glimpse of something I never thought possible. Handholding and lips touching and bodies shivering and legs interlocking. Oh, how a man's sexual energy really focuses the creative juices.

But the next night, I was visited by another princess, and the beauty beheld made the previous night's visitor seem a joke.

Night Two: Klara Le Roux

Klara wasn't born a girl, actually. She started life out as a passionflower, hidden atop a lone hill in the forests of northwestern Oregon. As Thomas Moore says:

> *'Tis the last rose of summer, left blooming alone*
> *All her lovely companions are faded and gone*
> *No flower of her kindred, no rosebud is nigh*
> *To reflect back her blushes and give sigh for sigh.*

But providence could not bear to let this one disappear.

One morning, as the summer was ending, a young family was hiking through the forest: Rylond and Mila Le Roux with their three-year-old daughter, Annika. The young couple strolled hand in hand while Annika frolicked, like a stock picture in a photo frame from Walgreens. Annika ran into the most beautiful flower she had ever seen. Heck, the most beautiful flower any of them had ever seen.

"That's a passionflower, Annika," explained Rylond. "They bloom for thirty-six to forty-eight hours, and then they disappear forever."

This made Annika weep uncontrollably.

"But I want her!"

So, they took the flower home, and Annika set the flower floating in a mason jar in between a large, uncut diamond and a picture of Mila's parents' wedding day.

The brilliance was set to die away that day. That night, as the bloom closed in on herself, a kaleidoscope of butterflies came from the diamond and swarmed the dead blossom, revealing a wailing child bathed in light. Rylond and Mila awoke and ran downstairs to see what was causing all the noise. When they saw the baby, their hearts went out to her. They gave her the name Klara, and thus she started her second life as a human being and grew to reign as Supreme Love Child of the Pure Hearted. Annika was excited to have a little sister, and no one ever suspected anything other than natural circumstances surrounding the child. The family of four lived happily on the side of a mountain, and sixteen years later, Klara visited me on that second night.

She arrived at my house in a beat-up old car at around eight that night. I brought out two CDs, *Frank Sinatra's Greatest Hits* and The Original West End Recording of the *Miss Saigon* soundtrack.

We drove to a concert because I was convinced I knew why I had failed on the previous night with Adalyn.

The solution is easy, Rosario, I told myself. *Since it didn't work out to go see a musical act by your favorite musical group, this time go to a concert of music by someone you've never even heard of.*

Ladies and gentlemen, I took Klara to a John Cage concert.

Listen to this: the first piece featured a man dripping a cup of water on the floor, followed by a lady beating an upright piano with a dead cat, followed by a five-hundred-pound man in a football helmet running screaming into the piano.

Applause.

The second piece featured a woman in a triple-extra-large blue denim shirt sitting in the middle of the stage. One man came on with scissors and cut a bit of the shirt off. Then another man. And another. And another. About twenty men surrounding this woman until you could no longer see her. She screamed.

Applause.

We did not stay for any more pieces.

Instead, we drove around the city and glittered in each other's presence. Parked the car on top of a familiar hill in the forests of northwestern Oregon. I took her in my arms, dancing slowly and closely to "The Last Night of the World." Her beautiful blue eyes were locked on mine, the fragrance of her flower essence stronger than anything.

We talked for hours. Her dreams, my ambitions. In the entirety of my short life up to that point, there was never such a night of clear-headedness. But like every night, this one was soon to end.

In fact, I could not believe what happened next. Going in for the kiss, a kaleidoscope of butterflies faded her away and the night ended. Just as she came into this world, so she left mine.

I would not see her again for many years, and the following daytime was marked by severe anger. How could I have failed with women two nights in a row? What was wrong with me? What darkness lies within the untrained man!

Of course, she ended up marrying my first human enemy, Mr. Arnoux Webber. We will not visit the story of Rosario and Arnoux just yet. Just know that for a time, hate knew no fury as that between us two men.

Consequently, life being the joker that it is, I have grown to truly love my enemy. His vision and sensitivities are so rare among Christian artists these days. My prayer for him is that he realizes the greatest use of a talent is to fight for it, in spite of the inner shouts of inadequacy.

I mean, for crying out loud, he married the Diamond of the Breath! He better make use of it!

Meanwhile, the third night was upon me, and I was given a last chance to come home from girl season with a prize.

Night Three: Naemi

Naemi and I spent the night eternally walking toward each other but never actually touched. Like two people on treadmills facing each other. Chasing the moon.

Yet I never felt closer to any living being. She was neither a star princess like Adalyn nor a passionflower like Klara, but in her simple humanity, she touched me deeper than most could ever claim to have known. It was at her berry farm where I learned the sweet scent of a woman. In times of trouble, my Diamond returns that fragrance and the beast is calmed. Her berry farm was also the home to many enchanted creatures, namely the powerful winged stallion named Tanyonta.

At the end of the night, Naemi and I rode upon Tanyonta through the clouds, shouting pranky things like "HO, HO, HO" and "MERRY CHRISTMAS" and "HE SEES YOU WHEN YOU'RE SLEEPING." Parents had lots of explaining to do the next day.

But as the sun rose on this, the third night of my Rhinemaiden visitors, a voice boomed from above the clouds.

"Choose her or choose the desert."

Not exactly fair. I shouted, *"Her! Oh my God, yes, her!"* I said it before my mind had a chance to catch up. I guess I don't know exactly if that was the right answer, and we'll never know really. Perhaps Tanyonta did not agree with the decision. Perhaps Naemi saw something I didn't. Perhaps back at the berry farm, a more worthy warrior had claim over this girl.

As the words escaped my mouth, I felt her body slipping. Before I had a chance to respond, Naemi was falling to her doom. I jumped to my doom to try and rescue her, but gravity said that wouldn't work. Only Tanyonta could save her now, which he obviously did. He shot past me and swooped her up. I assumed he would come back for me. But the ground was getting closer and closer and bigger and rounder and flatter and the trees were scraping my arms and the branches were breaking my fall and everything hurt and *bam* and *boom* and *bonk*.

I woke up in my bed.

But it was a new bed.

In Upstate New York.

I stayed there for twelve years.

ALL SALES
FINAL

THE HOUDINI MASSACRE

It could be an early spring morning as easily as a late winter after-noon in the slow heart of Upstate New York. Since he is never one for assumed politeness, Rosario barges into a pawn shop to keep warm while he waits for the bus.

"What a lodge of worthless garbage," he mutters. A 1940s Bakelite, ancient TVs Moses himself must have used. Behind the old man at the register, he sees a significant collection of glass hookahs. Behind the hookahs, a fishbowl.

"How much for the fishbowl?"

"Not for sale."

Challenge accepted, thinks Rosario. "Why not?"

Old man shrugs, takes a bite out of a pear. Says, "You know any magic?"

Rosario laughs. "Sure do. You got a deck?" His bus is sched-uled to come in two minutes, but there's always the next one.

Almost like he is expecting this, the old man pulls out a stale 52. He watches intently as Rosario performs the one card trick he learned a few years back. When he finishes, the old man's eyes light up. He leans back in his chair.

"I've seen that one before, of course. Still don't know how you magicians do it."

"So, why won't you sell the fishbowl?"

He coughs into his sleeve. "Oh, right. Well, honestly, I don't give two sleeves about the fishbowl. It's yours for free if you can help me though, magician."

Rosario smiles. He eats up weird interactions like this. *Guess I'm a magician now.*

"All right. You got twenty minutes. What do you need?"

The old man sits up straight, instantly appearing forty-five years younger.

"I knew this girl; her name was Lorena. We met at a pawn shop in 2001. I was never a—*cómo se dice 'Don Juan'*—but somehow, we hit it off. Turns out we both had a dream of one day opening a pawn shop. So, I got her phone number and we went on one date. I thought it would be cool to go to an old bookstore downtown together. Figure out if we liked the same stuff. Bad idea.

"Lorena immediately goes to the female authors' section and gets comfortable with *Wuthering Heights* or some crap. Meanwhile, I had recently gotten into magic, so I pick up a book of spells and try out my *encants*. Every couple of minutes I say to Lorena, 'Hey, check this out,' and fumble through a Pierce illusion or a Hawthorne blanket.

"I start to panic as I realize Lorena is much more interested in her 19th-century literature than in my birthday-cake magic tricks. I should have just stopped and, I don't know, gone to buy her a coffee or something. Instead, my romantic ass thinks to itself, *What this girl needs is to see some* real *magic.*

"I flip to the last trick in the book. 'The Houdini Massacre,' it was called."

The old man shrinks back and takes a bite out of his pear. Rosario is . . . expectant.

"After all these years, I don't know what happened, my boy. A blur of Marvel special effects and pink smoke. Next thing I know, Lorena is trapped in that fishbowl. It's been twenty years, and I've tried everything I can think of to get her out. Any ideas, magician?"

They stare at each other for a while. The old man looks just as ragged and lame as any other old man Rosario has ever seen. Literally just a pile of cholesterol waiting to die.

Eventually Rosario breaks the silence.

"How old *are* you?"

"Thirty-seven."

"Damn."

Another minute of silence.

"Sucks to suck, old man. I'm not actually a magician."

Then, with the confidence of a summer-camp counselor with a limited but potent collection of ukulele covers to use as currency in the forgiving hand job market, Rosario turns to the fishbowl and speaks.

"Nice face, honeylips. I'm headed to *The Nutcracker* this weekend; you can come with if you promise to be good."

He turns around to leave the store.

Silence.

The crunch of old teeth chewing on a pear.

Suddenly, he hears the soft *twing* of glass cracking. Everything inside Rosario screams at him to turn around.

Another *twing*. He keeps walking toward the exit.

A cute cacophony of shards hitting the floor. It *almost* makes him turn around—you know, to make sure the old man is safe.

He's at the door, pushes it open and feels the cold air, and stops. The next bus will be there soon.

"Best of luck," Rosario says over his shoulder.

He walks out, lets the door shut behind him.

But the door does not shut. He hears windchimes. He finally turns around and sees the most beautiful girl standing outside the pawn shop with a book in her hand and a confused look on her face.

She speaks. May God strike me down if every butterfly on the planet doesn't fly into Rosario's stomach at this moment.

"So . . . you like *Wuthering Heights?*"

UN DOTE PERDIDO

Applause.

Rosario Davez finishes another show. This one was a high school production of *Legally Blonde*, his honest-to-God favorite musical of all time. After the applause dies down, the orchestra begins the necessary exit music. (I mean, how awkward would it be for the parents to shuffle out of the auditorium in silence?) Rosario goes to town on the piano keys as he always does.

Two minutes later, most people have left the theater, and there aren't enough left to warrant a final round of applause for the orchestra. Sometimes, a musician's stray friend sticks back and does a solo, Shia Labeouf-style clap. No such recognition tonight.

This always slightly bothers Rosario. No matter what or where he performs, no matter the number of people listening or the style of music, he always gives so much. In terms of energy, no one could match the limitless joules emanating from this paramount in his early twenties. In terms of musical focus, he is unable to give a nonchalant performance. His mind is constantly evaluating every note and phrase as its own expression, as well as its place within the greater context of the piece. After all this effort, part of him is always frustrated at the lack of attention it gets.

I suppose it's narcissistic of me to want this, but sometimes it'd be nice if someone would tell me that they noticed what I do, Rosario always thinks.

After shows, the orchestra eats together at an Applebee's or some other microwave. He orders mozzarella sticks and is having trouble expressing his struggle tonight. The orchestra played great, they all agree. Even Tuba Jeff, who always struggles to keep up in the first act, did a decent job. Yet here is the peculiar pianist, going off about some nondescript issue.

"I guess I just don't know if there's a reason to be giving as much as I do. What's the point?"

"I get it, Rosario," says Daisy Wilkinson, the other pianist in the show. "I've been doing these shows for as long as you've been alive. Trust me, I get it. You wanna know the reality, though? We are nothing more than a glorified cassette tape."

"Cassette tape?" interrupts a violinist. "Is that what you and Moses used to listen to when you played together?" The table erupts in laughter.

"Okay, whatever." She smiles. "The point is, the best we can do is a good job, Rosario. And we did. We supported those kids and helped them have as close to a professional experience as most of them will ever have. Every time they got off the music, we were able to find them and fix it. We are . . ." She pauses to think, then starts again: "We are the musical equivalent of a good pair of sneakers."

"I swear to God, Daisy. What the hell are you talking about?" asks Tuba Jeff. More laughter erupts.

"No, really, Jeff! Think about this. Olympic athletes need the best equipment and gear and attire to do what they do, right? Even Usain Bolt, if he had on a cheap, broken pair of Adidas, wouldn't be able to run the way he does. Am I right?

"It's the same with these shows. Most of the time, these kids deal with terrible orchestras that don't follow well, are not loud enough when they need to be, and are overpowering at the wrong times. You know as well as I do, Rosario, how pianists usually can't do their jobs and end up leaving the poor kids high and dry on their solo numbers."

Rosario thinks back to a performance of *Rent* he saw where the girl playing Mimi gave her absolute all on "Out Tonight," but the band was so bare, she might as well have been singing a cappella.

"That's actually pretty good, Daisy," chimes in the conductor. "Rosario, you're the best pianist I know. I also understand your frustration. It's a shame we can't pay you guys more. But know that the kids and I appreciate you more than you can imagine. I don't say it as much as I should, and the kids are kids, so they're not even aware of how awesome you all are. But as *cliché* as it sounds, this show cannot happen without you all."

And on the night goes, every extrovert in the group sharing their experiences. Rosario stops complaining. These are good people. He is proud to be among them.

The next night, they do the same thing again, but this time, they go to TGI Friday's. Rosario orders mozzarella sticks again.

I've been doing these shows for as long as you've been alive.

The words that won't, can't leave Rosario's mind. He thinks of Daisy Wilkinson. He isn't sure, but she must be sixty-five. At least sixty. This year, Rosario has made around 35,000 or 40,000 dollars. He wonders if that's the amount Daisy Wilkinson makes. Not that he usually thinks of money, but it is still weird to think that a woman so much older would make the same amount of money as him. It is a thought he can't shake. How else could she make money at this point? All she does is play shows and accompany choirs and voice lessons. The same stuff Rosario does for money. Well, except accompanying dance classes, which is what Rosario is doing right now.

I've been doing these shows for as long as you've been alive.

Is this what Rosario's life is going to look like? Playing for high school musicals, community-theater orchestras, a band here and there? Every spring for the rest of his life, will he get the same calls asking him to sight-read another freshman trombone player's jury? Is this what he has 120,000 dollars of student loan debt for? The more he thinks of it, the more it terrifies him.

Is this all he is good for?

"And . . ."

Rosario hits a typical F major 7, his fingers faster than his brain. He has forgotten where he was for a minute there. No harm done: all his subconscious needs to know is the tempo and whether it's in three or two. He allows himself to be present in this moment, turning off any thoughts of old lady Daisy Wilkinson.

Accompanying dance classes used to be his dream job. Hang out with beautiful girls all the time, no music to read, just improvise for an hour. The same thing he did at home whenever he didn't have the patience or discipline to practice the classical stuff.

Conceptually, it was the greatest job he could imagine. One time, his colleague, Axle, shared with him a fulfilling perspective: "They applaud at the end of every class. It always seems to me like they are clapping for me. And why shouldn't they? I just created music from thin air, from my mind, my imagination. It is a gift that I can share only once, and these girls, they are the lucky recipients."

Rosario appreciates these perspectives, especially recently. The existential dilemmas are getting more frequent, sometimes triggered by phrases said in passing about the "starving artist" trope, other times triggered if none of the girls come up to him after a class and tell him he's awesome. In the few years he has been accompanying dance classes, he knows the joy he once felt is disappearing. This dream job of his is becoming more like a nightmare with each passing day.

"God, I'm so needy," he finds himself muttering.

"What was that?" asks the teacher.

"Oh, sorry. One more time?"

The dance teacher smiles kindly and nods. She claps her hands in a slow three-four tempo; Rosario takes his cue and plays another F major 7. He feels a tinge of embarrassment that he chose the same key as the previous combination. Then he chuckles. As if anyone would notice.

He wonders how dancers are always so kind. What an amazing lifestyle they lead, where their art is literally imbued into how they live. To truly express yourself as a dancer, you need to be in top physical shape, of course. But there is something more. Rosario remembers a time backstage walking in between the dancers as they warmed up. Stray feet were inches away from kicking him in the face, yet he never felt in danger. The girls were so aware of their bodies, they truly embody that age-old mom-ism of having eyes in the backs of their heads. Such a different world than the one Rosario occupies. As a pianist, he explores the infinite complexity of his hands and fingers, but they dance through the even more infinite complexity of their entire bodies.

"Thank you, Mr. Davez."

He snaps back to reality, jokingly slaps some keys, and ends his piece. The dancers all laugh, and the prettiest one smiles.

"If you are still with us," the teacher jokes. Zea is her name, and she is by far Rosario's favorite dance teacher to play for. She turns to the class. "Everyone put away the barres and return for center."

It is this part of the class Rosario both regrets and awaits every time. The girls take the ballet barres and walk past him to stack them in the back of the room. They smile at him. The prettiest one smiles at him.

"Good morning, Rosario."

"What's up," he says with a grin.

Every. Freaking. Time. What an awkward guy he is. He decides to be present for the rest of the class. His existential thoughts can be dealt with later.

And it goes on uneventfully. The girls run and jump across the floor to his Neapolitan-style waltzes. The air is thick with their panting. After about twenty minutes, everything slows down for the cooldown. This is the part of the class where he is allowed to play in any meter he wants. The part of the class that allows him to release all the creativity he has been holding back for eighty-five minutes. Hell, if it weren't for the cooldown, Rosario might quit music altogether. What is the point of it all, anyway?

He thinks to himself how freeing it is to not have to play to a specific rhythm. On top of the existential dilemmas, Rosario has also been growing a disdain for common practice tonal music. It's all so square, and he can't get away from it. In dance class, he can experiment harmonically and even shift phrase lengths within an overarching eight-bar phrase, but it always has to be in a typical meter: two-four, three-four, six-eight, et cetera. Screaming inside him is the reality that music isn't *only* meant to be danced to, and frankly, it's not like the dancers are exactly dancing to *his* music. Any other pianist playing in tempo would do. Heck, his colleague Axle just plays three congas, and that is good enough for them. Oh, and speaking of Axle, they're clapping right now . . .

"Great class, everyone. Thank you," says Zea. "And don't forget to thank Mr. Davez on your way out."

The applause intensifies as they all turn to him. He violently throws his hands up in a childish "ta-da!" gesture, once again fulfilling his class-clown duties and getting a smile from the prettiest one. He puts on his shoes and coat. Why does he always take off his shoes? Weirdass.

"Good job today, Rosario." It's her.

"Thanks, babe."

"Oh, that was *you* who music directed *Fiddler on the Roof?* Jasmine talked so much about you; all the kids really loved you. She said you were helpful and funny, so much better than that other guy . . . what was his name?"

"Lord Farquaad."

"What?"

"That was what the kids called him. Kilbourn was his real name, but he was short and kind of looked and sounded like Lord Farquaad from *Shrek*. I think it's hilarious."

"Well, they were glad to be rid of him, and when you came, she said everything just started running more smoothly and all the kids were so much more engaged. You really made quite an impression—you said your name was Fernando?"

"Ha, close. My name is Rosario Davez."

"Rosario. Rosario. Rosario," chants Veronica Bishop. She is a feisty woman, slightly younger than his co-pianist Daisy Wilkinson and with much more energy. Talking with her is like having seven conversations at once. They are talking for the briefest moment before the show starts (a coffeehouse cabaret at a private high school in Upstate New York).

In their short conversation, Rosario has found out Veronica's daughter, Jasmine, the girl who played Hodel in a production of *Fiddler on the Roof* Rosario recently music directed, will be performing tonight accompanied by Olivia, a music teacher Rosario has a crush on and has agreed to turn pages for, since it's the closest thing to a date he'll ever get with her.

"Okay, Rosario. So, what is next for you?"

"Well, I'm hoping to go for my master's degree at The Juilliard School next year in collaborative piano."

At the mention of Juilliard, Veronica Bishop finally stops her chatter, impressed. "My God. You must be incredible, then! My uncle was a concert pianist: he won second place in the Tchaikovsky competition the year Van Cliburn won."

"Wait a minute," interrupts Rosario. "Who was your uncle?"

"Well, I doubt you would know him, though I guess if you are going to Juilliard, you just might! His name was Walter Brennan."

"Your uncle was *Walter Brennan*?"

"My goodness, do you know him?"

"Yes, of course. We studied all the great pianists at Eastman! He got second place in the Tchaikovsky competition back in 1963! Your uncle is a big deal!"

And with that, the friendship of Veronica Bishop and Rosario is secured. Of course, he has made up all that stuff about knowing who Walter Brennan is. He doesn't know the year Cliburn won the Tchaikovsky was actually 1958. If you asked him why he lied, though, Rosario wouldn't say. He just tends to lie here and there to keep things interesting.

They keep chatting until the show starts. The cabaret is as boring a gig as any other Rosario has participated in, though it is the first time he hears music from *Spring Awakening*, which will later become one of his favorites. When it's time, he goes up and turns pages for Olivia (on his knees, because they don't have an extra chair and he has said he doesn't need one anyway). Afterward, he says goodbye to his crush without even attempting a kiss, though he does exchange contact info with Veronica Bishop.

The next day, Rosario receives a text message that will change his life:

"Hi, Rosario, an absolute PLEASURE to meet you yesterday. I told Jasmine we met, and she was so excited! You are truly one of her heroes. I wonder if we can get together this week. I have something that might be able to help you deal with those pesky college loans you were telling me about. Let me know when works for you. I am quite flexible."

"Oh yes, I know Veronica and her husband. They've had quite the success with their business."

Brigham Read is a man Rosario looks up to greatly. He is ancient and vaguely resembles a post-*Godfather III* Al Pacino. He is a man who, in Rosario's eyes, has wisdom beyond wisdom in both spiritual and musical education matters. He is also a local legend: everyone knows him, and he knows everyone. This affirmation from Brigham Read is all the encouragement Rosario needs to chat with Veronica Bishop.

He supposes that she is offering to give him money or a gig or something, but when they have lunch at the Wegman's later that week, she tells him about a business opportunity. Edison General, it's called. Veronica Bishop and her husband Theodore have been directors in the area for a few years and have built up something called "residual income," which is part of what she is offering Rosario today. The entire conversation goes over his head, but he still cannot get the idea out of his mind.

He studies and researches in the only way he knows how: Google. Despite all the websites calling Edison General a pyramid scheme and a scam, he finds himself discrediting all the negative information he finds. This is his opportunity. His chance to escape becoming Daisy Wilkinson, living a life playing musicals that are beneath him, where his only competition is PTA moms with kids in the shows. His chance to never again have to play for another dance class, his dream-turned-nightmare job which he feels is slowly killing his desire for music. His chance to make an income worth writing home about. His chance to only take the musical gigs he wants.

His chance to prove to himself and to everyone that music is *not* the only thing he is good at—which will legitimize his music even more, because it is only by transferring his musical skills that he is able to have success in any other field. Plus, now if he gets into the Juilliard School, he'll be able to afford it.

With that, a week later, he meets Veronica Bishop again at the Wegman's, signs the papers, and pays the franchise fees.

Ladies and gentlemen: Rosario Davez, Energy Rebate Specialist.

UN DOTE ENCONTRADO

Present

Yeesh.

It is July 18, 2021. The clock reads 3:07 p.m., and Rosario has just spent almost four hours on a video call with his long-time friend and mentor, Piers Noble. It has been another life-changing conversation that has led to a trajectory-redirecting decision. He gets up from his desk and goes to the kitchen to make himself a late lunch. As he picks up a bundle of green onions, he thinks about how he let himself drift so far away from his calling as a musician . . .

April 2016

It has been an interesting year so far. The audition at Juilliard went so well, Rosario has been accepted! The acceptance email comes while on vacation with his mom and sister in Florida.

"Congratulations! You have been . . ."

But Rosario doesn't need to read the rest. He has been anticipating this email for months, and after reading the first word, he knows he is set. That night, his family celebrates with a meal at their favorite restaurant, Red Robin.

He starts telling everyone of his acceptance and accepting accolades from everyone who knows how big a deal it is, but he keeps a professional composure because he is now a managing director with Edison General. Rosario has been working with Veronica Bishop at the company for a year now, and on top of his regular commissions, has built up a steady residual income of about twenty-five bucks a month. Not much, but that is three hundred bucks a year he will have for the rest of his life without having to do anything. Plus, his first customers have already received their rebate checks, which makes him feel pretty good about himself: he is making the world a better place.

The music job life, on the other hand, is pretty bad. He has tried his hand at being a full-time chorus teacher, and it's quickly destroying his soul. Even though he is putting in so much effort in with Edison General, he still isn't making enough to quit his dance class and voice lesson accompanist jobs. All this will soon change though—summer is approaching.

Summer is a fun time for obvious reasons, but especially for Rosario: every June and July, Rosario goes to some exotic place with the Army Band. This year they'll be hitting up Fort Elmendorf-Richardson in Anchorage, Alaska.

Present

Rosario smiles as he thinks of how much he used to look forward to those Army trips. He puts the green onions to the side as he takes the defrosted chicken out of the microwave, pats it dry, and begins to season it.

Some butter and curry today, I think.

The phone buzzes to alert him that someone liked some random Facebook post. He picks up the phone even as he thinks, *Don't get distracted, you have just made a big decision. Don't make yourself regret it.* He tells himself this as he realizes newsfeed scrolling has just stolen five whole minutes of his day. He wonders how one phone app has become such an addiction to him . . .

May 2016

He cannot believe his eyes.

There has to have been some mistake.

He immediately dials the number for Juilliard. He doesn't know who to reach out to or even what department; he just needs to talk to someone.

It's lunchtime. Rosario has just finished leading another chorus rehearsal. He is so miserable at this job, he doesn't even realize he hates it. Today has been especially painful: in Upstate New York, as soon as the weather warms up, any attempts at classroom management go out the window. To cheer himself up, Rosario has revisited his favorite email ever: his acceptance letter into The Juilliard School.

But this time, for the first time, he reads the whole thing.

Down to the part where he reads, for the first time, that the school requests an email reply confirming his intention of accepting a position in the school. Within a week.

He looks at the calendar. It has been well over a month since his vacation in Florida when he received the email. Panic begins to set in.

"Yes, I understand I was supposed to respond to the email, and I am responding now," he tells the person at the other end of the line.

"We're sorry, Mr. Davez. When we didn't hear from you, we assumed you had no interest in our offer. We had to give your spot to someone else."

"Give my spot to someone else? What do you mean?"

"The Juilliard School has a limited number of spots available for new students. We can't just accept everyone."

"But you already accepted *me*! I don't understand why—"

"Again, Mr. Davez, there is nothing we can do. You can always apply again next year."

Click.

Two minutes later, there is a student at the door.

"Mr. Davez, why did you give me a D on my participation grade yesterday? You can't do that! I sang my heart out! It was Alex that was misbehaving all class, not me! I don't get why you have to be like this, Mr. Davez."

Present

The pan crackles with the sound of onions and chicken rolling in his special butter cream sauce. Over the last few months, Rosario has become pretty good at cooking, if he does say so himself. He lowers the heat on the stove to a simmer and heads over to his keyboard. He dusts off the piano-vocal score to the opera he wrote between June 2016 and August 2017.

He begins to play the opening chords of Act One, Scene Two: "Oscar White's Soliloquy." It was the first bit of serious music he ever composed. Sure, there were small pieces here and there he had written for school, but never a fifteen-minute, Wagnerian-style aria, and definitely not an entire opera. He remembers how he justified its creation five years ago, when he was desperate to mask his feelings of inadequacy . . .

January 2017

"After wallowing in my own filth and urine for a month, I have decided to do something that will be even better than going to Juilliard: I'm writing an opera."

It's a fun project, for sure. The opera will be called *Adventure Gospel*, and it will be a fictitious retelling of the incredible true story of Christopher Knight, a man who spent twenty-seven years secluded in the woods of North Pond, Maine, and who survived by stealing food, clothing, and supplies from the nearby town.

Rosario surprises himself with his dedication to this work. When he isn't teaching (if you could call it that—Rosario sticks around the school as a pianist but gives up the chorus teacher position and doesn't miss it one bit) or accompanying dance classes (absolute torture now) or going to marketing appointments for Edison General, he is working on the opera.

It is about six months into this project when Rosario is mindlessly scrolling on the internet when he sees an interesting ad. The picture is of a guy flashing a smile and a thumbs-up to the camera, standing in front of a room of professional-looking people. It says, "Win Big in 2017!"

I could use a win, he thinks. Then, without even clicking on the ad, not realizing what it is, not even realizing it is an ad, Rosario writes something inspirational and shares it with his friends. It is about a week later when he actually clicks on it to see what the energy is all about.

Once inside and sold on whatever the ad is selling, Rosario meets a man named Piers Noble, a man who embodies everything Rosario wants to be. He is handsome, in shape, wealthy, and has a beautiful wife. He drips more charisma and exudes more leadership than anyone Rosario has ever met in his life.

Rosario is immediately drawn into what Piers Noble calls "The Extraordinary Society," a group of amateur Facebook marketers who are excited about life and welcome Rosario with open arms. Within the Extraordinary Society are people all over the world making money, and as stated in the ad, "winning big." Specifically, by selling fancy water purification systems. Rosario does everything Piers Noble says, plugs into the biweekly coaching calls, and loves every moment. Even if he doesn't make any money, the mental gains he is making are well worth his time.

Throughout all this, the opera continues to be a huge priority. He doesn't go a day without putting something down on paper, thanks to the lessons of consistency Piers Noble instills in him. He is a great mentor, full of love and patience and positivity. He encourages Rosario to follow his dreams and to let himself be as great as the universe needs him to be. For six months, Rosario observes everything Piers Noble does, taking notes and applying concepts to his own life.

Present

As he plays the last notes of "Oscar White's Soliloquy," he sits there in appreciative silence.

This is really good stuff, he thinks. *I should finish it now that I have the time.*

Then he rushes over to the stove. Lost in the music, Rosario has almost overcooked the chicken. By the grace of God, it is saved. He pours the mixture over a bed of rice and turns on *Saturday Night Live*'s "Weekend Update," the only place to get the news these days.

It's only sixteen minutes long. No distractions, Rosario. Just this segment, then it's time to get to work.

The comedic master duo of Michael Che and Colin Jost reminds Rosario of the great friends he has made. He takes a bite and cherishes every morsel in his mouth, leaning back in gratitude for all the great people in his life. He wonders how all of them will take the news of his recent decision.

July 2017

That summer, Rosario meets a man who will be his second Piers Noble. He meets him as part of a deal he has made with his current crush. She started working with this guy a few months before and has told Rosario about him a few times. As far as Rosario is concerned, she is wasting her time and working too hard.

He tells her, "Heck, come work with me and make more money with less effort. In fact, let's do this: I'll meet your guy, and then I'll introduce you to Veronica Bishop over at Edison General. You can decide for yourself which company is better."

So, the day comes. Rosario decides to meet at his go-to spot: a pizza place called Tehrani's.

An odd, beaver-looking man in his mid-thirties walks in.

"Are you Esmond Daniels?" asks Rosario.

The man hides his shock with a goofy smile. "Yes, I am. Are you the man who correctly guesses strangers' names?"

Rosario chuckles. He is going to try his best to give this guy a hard time.

Instead, Esmond Daniels and Rosario hit it off. They talk business, they talk music, they talk Jesus, they talk life. He invites Rosario to the office to talk more about working together and also invites him to a men's retreat that he refuses to call a "retreat" because "retreat" means "surrender," and this is a calling to action for men of God.

There have never been such instant best friends as Esmond Daniels and Rosario Davez.

He has never thought he would become a financial advisor. But like he was with Piers Noble, Rosario is attracted to Esmond Daniels's energy more than anything else. The "what" they are doing is not remotely as important as the "why" and the "with whom" they are doing it.

Where Piers Noble taught Rosario how to be successful with his thoughts, Esmond Daniels gives him practical skills of selling, communicating, networking, value-offering. Where Piers Noble showed Rosario a clear-cut path to success, Esmond Daniels shows him the way successful people think and approach situations. Plus, since Esmond Daniels is in the same city as Rosario while Piers Noble is all the way out in Colorado, they can spend considerable amounts of time together.

Within six months of working with Esmond Daniels, Rosario has obtained all the licenses and certifications to work in finance in New York. Within two years, he amasses over two million dollars in assets under management, and close to a hundred families and individuals trust him to manage their retirement accounts and life insurance plans.

Present

Rosario finishes his meal right as the last few jokes of *SNL's* "Weekend Update" end. He wonders how long it's been since he considered himself a musician.

Sure, between 2016 and 2021, Rosario spent his days driving between dance classes and voice lessons and various other musical engagements, but those were just meaningless occupations at that point. A necessary evil, you could say. His attitude toward these jobs was a mix of a teenager working at Wendy's and one of the men of the mind from Ayn Rand's *Atlas Shrugged*. He had even developed a problematic talent: that of being able to have fully present conversations via text message with his right hand while simultaneously playing the piano with his left. Once, before a meeting with a Webster millionaire, Rosario brought his laptop and created an asset strategy while accompanying a vocal technique class at the Nazareth College. It was a sort of active metaphor to his life, wanting to be a great businessman but burdened by the need to play music.

The teacher made him put away the laptop.

Many of his friends had cut ties with him during that time. Friends who used to look up to him as a musical genius hardly recognized the suit-wearing bigot who still hung around Upstate New York. Conversations with Rosario were a constant duel of wits: he crucified anyone who clung to the idea that music was the only way to spend a life.

No bother to him of course, as he seemed to find a new life guru every six months, not to mention a new community of highly motivated individuals that encourage his ascent to wealth. He first met Veronica Bishop with Edison General in the spring of 2016, then Piers Noble with Extraordinary Society burst into his life in the winter of 2017. The next summer, Esmond Daniels introduced a new career to Rosario that grew to be such a big part of his life that whenever people asked him about himself, he would answer proudly that he was a financial advisor.

It is now 5:07 p.m. on July 18, 2021. He has just made the decision to return to music. He has looked back at the last five years and thought how funny it was that it took this long to realize that being a musician would actually be a good way to spend his life. Not that he regrets the time away from music—a lot of it was good. He has learned a lot of valuable things, and met a lot of people who will be his most cherished relationships throughout the rest of his life.

July 2018

In the summer of 2018, Piers Noble introduced the idea of real estate as a way to round out his wealth-building strategy. So, for his twenty-sixth birthday, Rosario buys himself a house.

Unfortunately, he and Piers rarely talk anymore, as much of Rosario's time is spent working with Esmond Daniels and meeting with clients. The times they do talk, however, Rosario is impressed to find out about the success Piers Noble is having in the world of Kansas City real estate, so he figures he will try his hand at some deals on top of his financial advisory work.

Esmond Daniels tries to warn him about putting too much on his plate, but at this point in his life, Rosario is king of the hill and nothing can bring him down.

Of course, there is a mountain of suppressed pain in there as well, but as far as he is concerned, emotional work is a hoax. So, though he has flown through 2017 and 2018 feeling on top of the world, gifted with a Midas touch, it won't be long before Rosario Davez finally breaks.

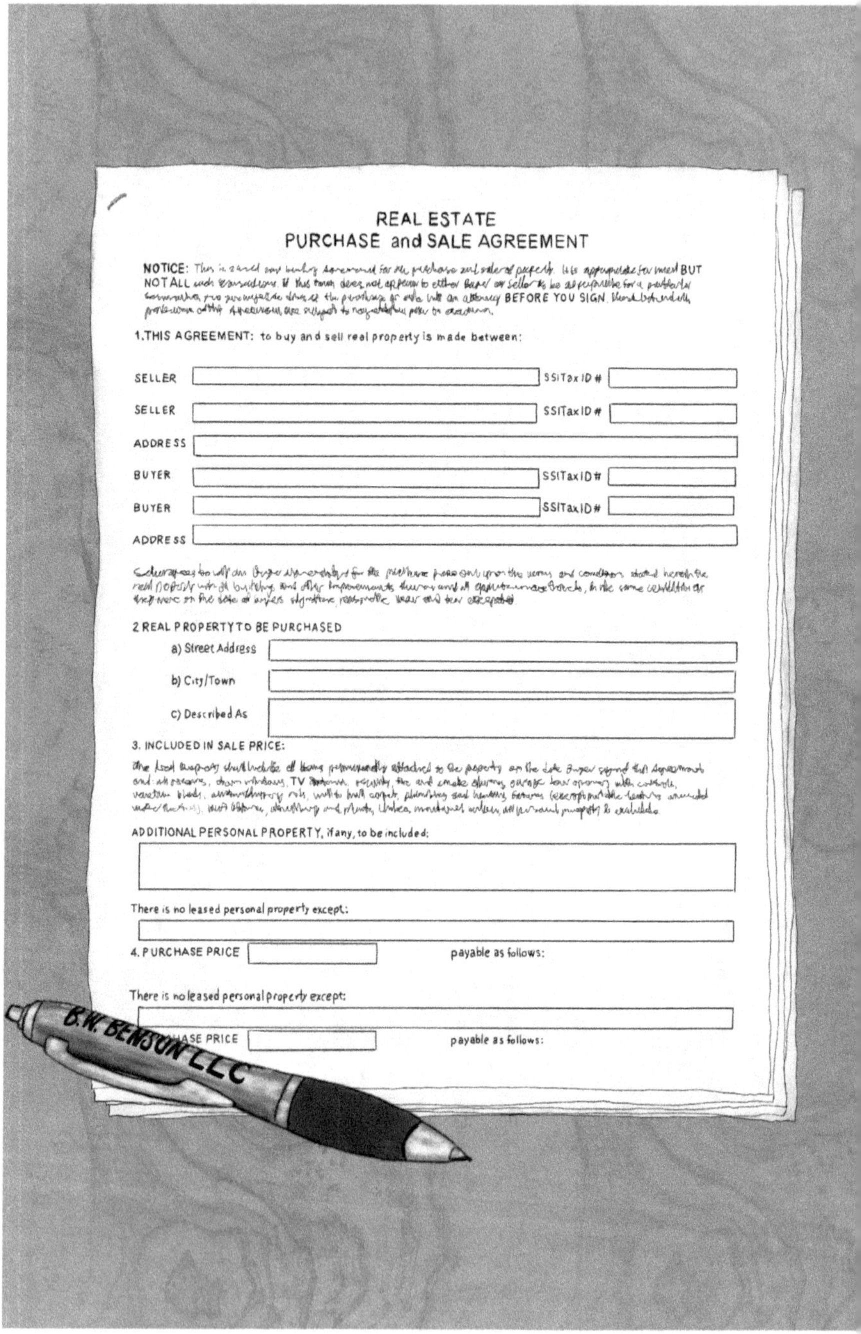

REAL ESTATE
PURCHASE and SALE AGREEMENT

NOTICE: [handwritten, illegible] ... **BUT NOT ALL** [handwritten, illegible] ... **BEFORE YOU SIGN**. [handwritten, illegible]

1. **THIS AGREEMENT:** to buy and sell real property is made between:

SELLER [____________________] SSITax ID # [________]

SELLER [____________________] SSITax ID # [________]

ADDRESS [____________________]

BUYER [____________________] SSITax ID # [________]

BUYER [____________________] SSITax ID # [________]

ADDRESS [____________________]

[illegible]

2. **REAL PROPERTY TO BE PURCHASED**

    a) Street Address [____________________]

    b) City/Town [____________________]

    c) Described As [____________________]

3. **INCLUDED IN SALE PRICE:**

[illegible]

ADDITIONAL PERSONAL PROPERTY, if any, to be included:

[____________________]

There is no leased personal property except:

[____________________]

4. **PURCHASE PRICE** [________] payable as follows:

There is no leased personal property except:

[____________________]

[PURC]HASE PRICE [________] payable as follows:

BUYING HOUSES AND OTHER HEADACHES

Thus, dear reader, we come to the beginning of Rosario's partnership with one Emerson Benson, local real estate mogul. In the winter of 2018–2019, Rosario is doing some research online when he finds a house for sale for only 9500 dollars in a rough part of downtown. He gives the owner a call. Emerson Benson picks up. They chat for a while and shoot the breeze as if they were old friends.

"You seem like a legit guy," says Emerson. "Come on to the office tomorrow morning: 681 Portland Ave. You drink coffee?"

"Hell, no. But I'll bring the donuts, how's that?"

"All right, buddy. See you in the morning."

Now, you should know, dear reader: Upstate New York winters are rough. So, when you get to the address of an office and no one answers the door, you don't wait around.

If only that were the end of it.

Later that day, Rosario gets a call from a Damon Houle, executive assistant to Emerson Benson.

"Hi Rosario. My name is Damon; I work with Emerson. Sorry about the miscommunication this morning—a crisis at one of the properties took him away and he was unable to meet with you."

"No problem, Damon. Thanks for calling."

"Sure, sure. Listen, after your phone call with Emerson, he wanted me to reach out to you and see if you'd be interested in an expanded offer on the house at Eiffel Place."

"What do you mean?"

"Well, to tell you the truth, he probably doesn't want me to talk to you about this but check it out: Emerson has just had a baby."

"Oh, wow. Congratulations."

"Yeah, yeah, it's great and all but . . ." Damon pauses, looking for the right words. "Emerson's not a . . . young guy anymore. He's been wanting to get out of New York for a long time, and now that he's a daddy again, he's desperate for a way out."

"Got it. So, he's looking to unload all his properties."

"Right. Well. Not exactly. He's looking for a partner to manage the company while he moves to Oklahoma. If you're interested, come by the office in an hour and we can go over the details."

"I'll see you in a bit, Damon."

The deal looks like this:

Eight properties, all but one within the 14621 zip code.

After-repair value of all properties: $670,000.

Estimated cost of repairs: $50,000–$100,000.

Expected rental income from all properties: $9800 per month.

The purchase amount of $180,000 from Rosario to BW Benson LLC will grant him a 49 percent ownership of the company as well as its two sister companies: Benson Heating & Cooling and Benson Properties.

All eight properties are currently owned and managed by these companies.

Half of the purchase amount ($90,000) will be treated as a loan from Rosario to BW Benson LLC, which will be paid back to Rosario at a one percent interest rate over the course of ten years.

Seems like a pretty good deal, right?

It makes sense, don't you think?

The properties all need a lot of work, and only one of them is producing a measly nine hundred fifty dollars in monthly income. Emerson Benson is bleeding money right now, having to pay off these mortgages and the ridiculous New York State property taxes.

Benson Heating & Cooling gets plenty of work to keep Emerson Benson and the crew busy, as well as providing income for all three companies not to go belly-up. But you can see how Emerson Benson really just needs two things to get out of this paycheck-to-paycheck cycle: an infusion of cash and a partner.

Meanwhile, Rosario is at a point in his music career where he is desperately looking for a way to never play the piano again. The chemistry he used to have with the dance teachers is long gone, and no one is hiring him to play shows anymore out of fear that he will use the contact to try to sell his vast range of services.

As far as he is concerned, all he has to do is get some money to Emerson Benson, give him and the team a few months to get all the properties habitable and rented, and Rosario is looking at an early retirement with a residual 4800 dollars a month, which will more than cover his own mortgage and lavish lifestyle.

Alas, Rosario doesn't entirely have 180,000 dollars. In fact, he doesn't even have 10,000 dollars to his name. What he does have, however, is OPM.

What is OPM?

Oh, just something they say in the real estate investment world: Other People's Money.

Now, this is not entirely legal, especially considering the heavy regulations on financial professionals working in the USA. But again, as far as Rosario is concerned, he has a means of getting that money. Namely, his own father.

A few months earlier, Rosario was amazed at how easy it was to convince Brahman Davez to hand over the management of his retirement funds. Now, all he has to do is convince Brahman to let him take half of the money for a once-in-a-lifetime legacy partnership.

The question is, should he? Should Brahman let his son invest his money? Should Rosario break financial regulations restricting the use of client money for personal investment?

From what you have read about Rosario up to this point, what do you think? Does he seem like a man who does his due diligence?

He is certainly a man who *thinks* he is doing his due diligence. He calls his friend Gloria, a real estate paralegal who is also an accomplished opera singer.

"Hey Gloria, I'm thinking of buying some rental properties, but I think I'm also going to be buying into half of a company. You know any lawyers who specialize in this sort of thing?"

"I know just the guy," says Gloria. "His name is Cade White; he's a good friend. I'll have him call you. Be nice to him, okay?"

"Never in a million years. Thanks a lot, Gloria; you're the best."

Rosario sends Cade the information on the deal and Emerson's contract, as any good real estate investor would.

But you and I both know, don't we? Rosario's already made up his mind on this, hasn't he?

Cade is a good lawyer and does his best to warn Rosario.

"What do you know about these guys? Do you have any experience working with them? Have you any experience in real estate? Where did you get these numbers, and how do you know they are accurate? How do you know you can trust this Emerson Benson guy to keep up his end of the bargain? Have you even visited these properties?"

After a few years working as a financial advisor, Rosario knows how to answer all these questions in a calm, politician-type manner. Cade isn't at all convinced but agrees to hop on a phone conference with Rosario and Damon once the papers are ready to be signed.

It is a few weeks later. The snow is thick. The cold, cold February that usually reminds Rosario of his pathetic singleness hardly bothers him this year because he is about to be a real business owner complete with an office, properties to manage, and passive income.

The check from his father is ready. It is for 45,000 dollars, made out to BW Benson LLC, the first of four equal payments spread out over four years.

Cade decides within a week of discussing the deal with Rosario that this is not a transaction that he wants any part of. Apparently, neither does Emerson Benson's lawyer, who, on the day of signing, sends out an email to all parties involved saying that he too is washing his hands of the deal.

Rosario isn't concerned. *What could go wrong?* he thinks. *I have a contract here. If there is a breach in any capacity, I can just sue, right? Isn't that how it works? Besides, I don't see what the benefit of them breaching the contract would be. All Emerson Benson needs is money, and he can get the team out to the properties.*

He has recently met the team. It was around lunchtime some Tuesday in late January. Emerson Benson had everyone come to the office to meet Rosario.

"Everyone, this is your new boss," he said. "In the next couple of weeks, Rosario is going to be signing on as my partner. You are to do anything he says as if it were coming from me."

It was probably the proudest moment of Rosario's life, hearing another man talk about him with such power, such prestige. The team was a scroungy bunch of construction types, but they seemed respectful and hardworking.

Emerson's cool. Besides, what kind of loser would take 45,000 and run, leaving behind a perpetual income stream of 5,000 bucks a month? he thinks as he looks at the signature block of the contract.

One month after the papers are signed, repayments on the loan from Rosario to BW Benson LLC are to begin. The monthly repayments will only be around one hundred and eleven dollars for the first year. If that seems small, remember half of the 180,000 will be paid back to Rosario at one percent over ten years. Since he only paid half of the 90,000 dollars, Emerson Benson won't start the full repayment plan immediately.

Is this starting to make sense, dear reader? The absolute pig-shit sandwich that Rosario has signed himself into?

The first three repayments come in with no hassle. Right around June of 2019, however, communicating with Emerson Benson starts to become its own brand of torture. Calls are not returned; no one is at the office.

Now, don't get me wrong. Every time they do talk, Emerson Benson is very apologetic.

"Hey Rosario, so sorry for the delay. Things are absolutely crazy right now. We have to schedule a time to get together, you and me, partners' meeting. How's this Friday?"

"That'll work, but let's make sure this one actually sticks, okay?"

"For certain, brother."

And of course, Friday comes, and the call goes unanswered. This happens five times before a meeting finally occurs during the hopeful month of August.

They meet at Emerson Benson's Hamlin estate, a ghetto-ass mansion as can hardly be described.

Rosario pulls into a circular driveway and sees the immaculate landscape. Ten-foot-tall hedges surround the land to provide privacy from the outside world. As he gets out of his car, Emerson

Benson himself comes out from the house, gives Rosario a big hug, and welcomes him to his getaway, his little piece of freedom. The two of them get into a golf cart so he can give a proper tour.

Driving around the property, he points out the pool—"Did you bring your swimsuit?" Then, he looks at the sky: "Well, probably not today, looking like rain later. But soon."

He parks next to a big patch of land next to the house and tells Rosario the history of the neighboring building, an edifice of historic significance, apparently. Continuing on foot through the badminton court and back to the main house, Emerson Benson's wife comes out and offers the men a drink. She is a lovely woman with a lovely smile, save the cigarette-ravaged teeth. He sips on the delicious passionfruit-flavored beverage as their little girl of two years runs out to her papa. He picks her up and they squeeze together all their love.

"This is Katie. Say hi to Rosario, Katie."

She utters a shy "Hi," then buries her face into her daddy's shoulder out of embarrassment. He throws her up in the air, catches her, then looks deep into her brown eyes.

"Rosario and I need to talk business, okay, sweetie?"

"Okay, Daddy. I love yooou."

"I love you too, princess. Run to your mama, now."

Little Katie runs away, and Emerson Benson turns to Rosario. "All right, my friend. We're finally here. Let's have that talk."

It has been six months since the paperwork was signed and Rosario and Emerson Benson's partnership officially began. They are both eager to talk, especially Rosario, who needs more than anything to know exactly what is being done with his 45,000 dollars.

Emerson shows him a list of figures that don't make a lot of sense to him. Rosario attributes his confusion to the fact that even after investing 20,000 in a real estate education program, he doesn't actually know the first thing about real estate. (Not that he would ever admit that to anyone.) Still, at the end of the conversation, there's no doubt that the 45,000 is gone. Instead of going into renovations, it went to pay back taxes and liens.

"Wait, so how much money do we have to renovate the properties?" asks Rosario.

"Well, until your next payment of 45,000, we don't have anything."

"That's not for another six months, Emerson. What are we doing for income now?"

"Benson Heating and Cooling has—"

"Yes, I know about Benson Heating and Cooling, and I don't give a crap about Benson Heating and Cooling. Why didn't you use the money like we intended so we could have the properties ready to go?"

"I never said that's what we would do with it."

"Goddammit, Emerson. Would you rather have debt *and* income, or neither debt nor income? Why is this the first I'm hearing of this?"

"I know. It's taken so long for us to finally talk. I'm sorry, but—"

"What do you mean, it's taken so long for us to finally talk? I've been trying to get this meeting to happen for months! And what have you been doing? Renovating your own house!"

"Look, Rosario, I need a *partner*, not some kid who doesn't have a clue about what's going on."

"How am I supposed to know what's going on when you don't answer your calls?"

"I'm *busy*, okay? Right now, we've got projects all over the city, and I don't have the men to do them, so I'm working overtime!"

"Okay! Now we're getting somewhere, Emerson. Let's get these projects taken care of so we can start turning over some profit within the next six months. What do we have going on?" He looks at the list of figures that don't make sense. "What is this by 242 Durnan Street?"

"I'm thinking of selling that one. The realtor says we can get at least 50,000 for it since it's already cash-flowing."

"Okay, hold on, let's think about this. Does it make sense for us to unload the one property that is making us money?"

"Well, if we get 50,000 from selling it, we can use that money get the other properties ready."

"True, but how long will that take?"

"Oh, not long. Weaver just needs drywall and flooring. Clifford, same thing. Goodman and Eiffel need a lot more work, but—"

"But we can deal with those later. And with Weaver and Clifford producing income, we're looking at what, 1850 a month?"

"Yeah, that's reasonable."

"Okay, what does your schedule look like tomorrow?"

The next day, Emerson Benson, Rosario, and a crew member named Isaiah go to 242 Durnan Street to paint the garage and get it pretty for realtor pictures. Rosario would rather pay some kid a hundred bucks to chip away old paint, but they still have a good time. All the while, Rosario reminds himself, *Hey, at least I don't have to play the piano anymore.*

And with that, the hopeful month of August 2019 ends . . . well . . . hopefully. Everything is set up for Emerson Benson and Rosario Davez to turn this miscommunication hiccup into a profitable venture. Now, I know you may have been expecting this to be the moment that Rosario breaks, but don't worry.

It's coming.

Be patient!

A MARRIAGE SANDWICH ON DEPRESSION BREAD

CECILIA: We met in the spring at a church Bible study called Institute.

ROSARIO: If you asked us today what we studied that night, I don't think either of us would be able to say. Too busy looking at each other the whole night.

CECILIA: I got his number, but apparently, he lost mine?

ROSARIO: Yeah, I was pretty good at putting my number into girls' phones back then. But we all know social media is where it's at, so the next day, I add her on Facebook and begin to invite her to FHE almost every week.

FHE: Family Home Evening. Every Monday, the Latter-Day Saints (LDS) of the Genesee Valley Branch would get together to

*play games, eat snacks, and share life together. Rosario organized the
weekly event.*

CECILIA: I would never go. I really didn't like people my
own age, plus it was a good hour drive to get downtown,
so despite the cute boy in charge of FHE, it wasn't really
worth it for me.

ROSARIO: We wouldn't see each other again until the
Hill Cumorah Pageant that summer.

*Hill Cumorah Pageant: The Book of Mormon, another testament of
Jesus Christ, was discovered by the prophet Joseph Smith in golden-
plate format, buried in a hill in Upstate New York. To commemorate
this book and its discovery, Latter-Day Saints from all over the country
make the pilgrimage to Palmyra, New York, every summer to partake
in what has become known as the world's largest outdoor theater event,
the Hill Cumorah Pageant.*

CECILIA: I had been living with my good friends, the
VanGorders, for a few months, and we had gone to see
the pageant several times that year already. It was the end
of the last performance of the season, when wouldn't you
know it? Coming down the aisles was that guy I had met
at Institute a few months earlier!

ROSARIO: I remember seeing her and getting so excited!
We get in a strong embrace, and then as she introduces
me to her friends, we continue standing in a side hug. I
tell you, man, her skin was *so* soft.

CECILIA: He invites us to get ice cream that night. I politely decline on behalf of everyone—we've got a long drive home.

ROSARIO: Over the next few months, I keep inviting her to FHE to no avail. Can't quite say what it is, but I don't think she seems very interested in having fun.

CECILIA: Yeah, not really. Not that type of fun at least. I'm more of a "take a long hike through the Adirondacks alone" kind of girl. That fall is when I start dating Matthew.

ROSARIO: That fall is when I stop inviting Cecilia to FHE.

CECILIA: Yeah, right. You didn't stop!

ROSARIO: Okay, fine. But for your information, I got into serious dating mode myself around that time.

CECILIA: Here we go again . . . "I dated, like, one girl a week!"

ROSARIO: It's true! Most didn't turn into second dates, and even fewer went on after that. But if I was anything, I was consistent.

CECILIA: Anyway . . . we reconnected over Mutual on January 8, 2020. I said, "Hey I know you."

Mutual is the LDS dating app.

ROSARIO: I remember that morning so clearly. I had just gone to interview for a chorus accompanist position at a swanky Upstate New York high school. As expected, I nailed it. Even saw that my favorite dance teacher Zea's daughter, Ella, was going to be one of my students. Friends everywhere!

CECILIA: Just don't tell them about how you got fired from that other high school for dating a student . . .

ROSARIO: C'mon! *She was eighteen.*

CECILIA: Hah!

ROSARIO: Anyways, eventually I got Cecilia to come over to my house. It was honestly kind of an awkward date in every respect. We never really had much chemistry, did we?

CECILIA: I mean, not really. Not that we hated each other, obviously, but it all just happened so fast. We were more infatuated with each other than anything. Like, you threw a cookie at me, and within ten minutes, we were making out on your sofa.

ROSARIO: I had told Cecilia to bring over some desserts for our first date. She brought some old-person sweets. That should have been the ultimate red flag!

CECILIA: I remember you walking me through your house. You played your grand piano for me, then showed me all your paintings, and then the fire pit outside, introduced me to each of your nine fish, then finally the hot tub in the three-season room. It was a good house!

ROSARIO: You're right about that. See, the home tour is an important part of any date. For instance, if you're at a club and you're building up excitement for the after-party, you gotta make sure the energy is high both with the girl you're pulling that night as well as with everyone you're not. When you get a whole group to come to the house, you say something like "Okay, here are the rules: shoes off, shots, and no vomiting." Then the tour needs to be designed so that at the end, everyone's in front of the TV watching some movie or playing some games, maybe a Nerf gun fight, so that they are entertained while you continue the tour with the girl into your room.

CECILIA: Okay, thanks for that, you weirdo. What did that have to do with our date?

ROSARIO: Sorry, thought it would be helpful for the single boys out there.

CECILIA: We're talking about us right now!

ROSARIO: Right, right, right

CECILIA: So anyway, we start dating and go internet official just three days later on January 11, 2020. The day before Rosario gets promoted to Staff Sergeant with the Army Band.

ROSARIO: I think having Cecilia there at the ceremony was the first time I saw her as any sort of wife material.

CECILIA: Aw, so sweet.

ROSARIO: It was also around that time that I began work at Sutherland.

CECILIA: The time *we* began work at Sutherland. Remember, you thought it'd be a good idea for us to work at the same place? And every time you made a sale, you would get a candy and then come give it to me?

ROSARIO: It was literally the worst call center job. People would call in to cancel their AT&T subscriptions and our job was not only to convince them not to, but to also sell them some other product, primarily internet and cell phones.

CECILIA: It was while we were there we decided to get married. For . . . convenience reasons.

ROSARIO: Right, convenience.

CECILIA: Mormons don't support the notion of living together outside of marriage, to say nothing of their views on sex before marriage.

ROSARIO: So yeah. Convenience. We would be married and living together, we could go to work together, and at the end of the day, go home and do marriage things together.

CECILIA: It was a doomed plan from the start. I didn't last long at the call center, quit after about a month. Then I started working at a few places before landing a manager position at a home decoration retail company called At Home. That's when I started being the breadwinner.

ROSARIO: Can't argue with that. I stayed at the call center for six months before deciding to go full time as a financial advisor.

CECILIA: And you had given up on the real estate around then too, right?

ROSARIO: Oh no, that was way before. Emerson Benson disappeared back in September of 2019. I found out from Damon Houle that he had moved to Dallas, Texas. I tried contacting the guy, but it was radio silence. As I tried to get info on our properties, I found out that 242 Durnan Street did end up selling—not that I ever saw any of that money. The last we spoke, Emerson Benson had intentions of quitclaiming the houses completely into my name.

Quitclaiming is the process by which the owner of a property signs over all rights to someone else without officially selling it. This is common among family members and business associates.

ROSARIO: Needless to say, that never happened. Likely, this was a godsend. I took my friend Daniel Lane on a tour of the properties one day and he said, "Listen Rosario, even if you gave me these properties for free, it would take years to turn a profit on them."

CECILIA: Wow. They were that bad, huh?

ROSARIO: It was a disaster. I thought my depression after the Juilliard fiasco was bad. Compared to this, 2016 was a pleasure cruise. The fall of 2019, I finally broke. All my dreams of residual rental income seemed completely unattainable. I had one tenant at my property on Coronado Drive where I had my primary residence, but the tenant only covered a third of my mortgage. I had lost my father's money, which he had trusted me with. I had trusted Emerson Benson to be a worthy business partner, only to have my trust taken advantage of. It was a painful lesson to learn, and for a few months, my entire worldview was under attack. What was the point of being nice anymore? Friendly people don't get ahead; tigers and vultures get ahead. Not that I became either of those. From September to January, I got fat. Barely left my house, hardly did any work as a financial advisor, too depressed. How hypocritical to even think about helping people with their money. It was the lowest point of my life so far . . . and then I met Cecilia.

CECILIA: Aw, no pressure!

ROSARIO: You really lifted me out of it, Cecilia. I'll always love you for that.

CECILIA: Okay, okay, okay, I guess I'll come out and say you helped me get out of a funk too. I had broken up with that Matthew guy in the fall of 2019 and gone into a promiscuous phase for a few months. I was depressed and struggled with anxiety and self-harm. I don't think I realized it at the time, but Rosario was probably one of the best things that ever happened to me up to that point, for at least the first couple of months of our dating and marriage.

ROSARIO: Yeah! Thanks for sharing that, Oats.

CECILIA: You're Oats, not me!

ROSARIO: B-b-b-but . . .

CECILIA: So, when we got married, Rosario taught me the word for husband in Spanish: *esposo*. I started expanding it through a variety of mouth sounds in a pattern something like "espos-et-oat-et-it-oats" and this made him laugh so much, eventually we just shortened it to Oats. Which is why *he* is Oats, not me!

ROSARIO: I love it. We had some good times, didn't we?

CECILIA: Some, yeah . . .

ROSARIO: Like one time, we went camping. Cecilia is very much in her element out in the country, away from buildings and people and all that city life that I love so much.

CECILIA: I had been wanting to take him out to the Adirondacks for such a long time. We would go on nature walks here and there, but what I really thought we should do as a couple was go on big hikes and stuff. The summer of 2020, we finally made the trip and climbed Mt. Ampersand.

ROSARIO: It was a memorable trip, for sure. Uh, but to put it simply, I was just not built for the outdoors.

CECILIA: You think?

ROSARIO: Cecilia had the amazing instinct to pack our food. You wanna know what she packed?

CECILIA: Fruit gummies, fruit cups, Scooby Snacks, a can of olives, and hot dogs. What's wrong with that?

ROSARIO: Hah! I was *dying*! On the car ride back, Cecilia got the instinct to stop at a McDonalds. You know, to assuage my requests for real food.

CECILIA: I'm so proud.

Rosario sighs, they both smile, and there is a moment of silence between the divorced pair.

CECILIA: Well, I guess we better get to the part no one wants to talk about.

ROSARIO: Yeah.

CECILIA: I didn't really think we were going to get divorced. I just needed some space at first.

ROSARIO: It was a Sunday in October of 2020. Cecilia didn't want to go to church that day; she told me to go alone, which I did. Because of the pandemic, we had never actually attended our home ward in person, but my old ward, the GVB YSA, was holding meetings, so I went to that service.

Latter Day Saints refer to their religious gathering places as wards. Wards are assigned based on proximity, unless you are a YSA, a Young Single Adult. Between the ages of eighteen and thirty, YSAs meet at their own designated gathering places, the intention being for them to meet other YSAs and get married. Rosario was baptized at his designated YSA gathering place, the Genesee Valley Branch (GVB) before marrying Cecilia, so most of his LDS friends were in regular attendance there.

ROSARIO: When I returned home from church, Cecilia had taken most of her stuff and left the house.

CECILIA: The night before, I called my dad to bring his truck over in the morning to help me move my stuff out of our house. Like I said, I needed some space. Honestly, though, it wasn't the first time I had done this. Pretty much every time I was finished with a relationship, I would just pack up and leave with no warning.

ROSARIO: And I knew that, too! Of course, I was convinced it wouldn't happen to me. But there I was, standing in my living room with this stupid look on my face, holding my phone like an idiot. I give Cecilia a call. No answer.

She texts me, "I'm okay, I'm at my dad's. Just need some space." I start panicking.

CECILIA: Rosario wasn't a bad husband. We just had fallen into a funk, you know? Communication was really difficult.

ROSARIO: That's a really loving way to say that I liked to lie about *everything*.

CECILIA: Well, okay. But you said it, not me!

ROSARIO: Damn right.

CECILIA: While we were apart, it just kind of dawned on me that I didn't love him anymore. I didn't even *like* him all that much. He was manipulative and abusive. Not in a dramatic or violent or scary way, but even if it was casual, it was still a problem. Also, all my friends thought he was weird. Also, it was like he was always in a "trying to sell life insurance" mode. Not attractive. Hella awkward.

ROSARIO: The rest of that Sunday was a blur. I must have called a mentor or something. No one teaches you what to do when a wife leaves.

CECILIA: You wrote me a song, remember? Sent me a video of you playing it along with the lyrics.

ROSARIO: Oh my gosh. Yes, I did. "Your Heart," it was called. Beautiful song. Looking back though, even that was kind of a manipulative move. Don't you think?

CECILIA: No, I don't think so. That was nice. What was manipulative was you writing my dad a letter!

ROSARIO: Gawd, what a dork I was. But I didn't know what to do!

CECILIA: Me neither. I just kept working. Was tired all the time because my company was piling the hours on my schedule, and they even started sending me to other stores all over the Northeast to fix their messes.

ROSARIO: I still think that is so cool. You're going to freaking own the company one of these days.

CECILIA: It was on one of these trips that I saw Rosario again—this was after we'd been separated for a good six months. My company had sent me to Wayne, New Jersey at the same time he was at Fort Dix, New Jersey. We spent one night together at my hotel. It was . . . nice. But despite our best efforts, the feelings were not there anymore. I think we both put a lot of pressure on ourselves and each other to create a marriage that was incongruent with reality. That's probably why it took over two years for us to finally sign the divorce papers.

ROSARIO: I had so much shame around the idea of divorce. *That'll never happen to me,* I always thought.

CECILIA: Same. But the fact of the matter is we didn't really know each other. Some people will blame our faith for the rush into marriage, but I think we can both take responsibility for rushing into something neither of us really knew anything about. I mean, we dated for two months and then got married. Our whole relationship lasted a little over nine months.

ROSARIO: A marriage sandwich on depression bread.

CECILIA: What?

ROSARIO: I mean, we were both in a depression before meeting each other, then we had a solace of a few good months together before plunging into a depression again.

CECILIA: Yeah, that sounds about right. So, how did you get over your post-separation hump?

ROSARIO: Turn the page, baby.

BAPTISM

A rush of cold water.

Freezing cold water.

Rushed, short breaths.

The newly separated Rosario tries to calm his body down. It is shivering and there is nowhere he can go within the tiny shower to get away. This is how he's going to shower from now on.

It'll get easier.

He turns off the shower to apply the soap, trying to convince himself he's doing this to be economical.

If you think about it, we probably waste more soap if we lather while the water is running. Plus, this way, the soap has the chance to really seep into the skin before getting rinsed off.

He then proceeds to spill an inarguably ridiculous amount of bodywash.

Dammit.

Two minutes pass. He is sufficiently soapy.

Here we go.

The rush of freezing cold water is even worse this time. He has a theory that despite it being the dead of winter in Upstate New York, the water in the house is at a baseline warmer temperature, which explains how that initial hit of water wasn't as bad. This new surge of water has been sitting in a frozen state, ready to pounce and to show no mercy.

More rushed, short breaths.

It'll get easier.

The whole affair takes less than five minutes. He gets out of the bathroom. Yana Goldenseal, his friendly neighbor who has graciously offered her house as a halfway home, shouts from the kitchen.

"Everything all right?"

"Oh, you heard that did you?"

They both laugh. "Why, Rosario? Just, why?"

"I take cold showers now."

He can almost hear her rolling her eyes from across the house. "Weird ass."

After Cecilia moved out, Rosario was left alone to deal with the realtors, buyers, closing, et cetera. Originally, they had wanted to sell it together: the whole affair was his idea of a romantic gesture. *We'll leave the suburbs and move to the country where we can raise the kids and be a cool family.*

Now that his wife is gone, he wishes he hadn't rushed into this decision. But then again, when has he not rushed into a decision?

He joined the US Army after a bad breakup his sophomore year of college. He became an Energy Rebate Specialist and Financial Advisor overnight, because . . . because why not. Between 2012 and 2019, he bought and lost five cars. He bought the first house he found because he thought people would admire it. He invested 20,000 dollars in a real estate education program and then lost close to 50,000 dollars of his father's money to Emerson Benson by ignoring everything he learned in said education program. He married a girl after two months of dating her.

He is now selling his primary residence after only two years. In less than three months, he will lose all of the 15,000 dollars in equity he earned from selling that house, spending it on coaching programs and marketing strategies for his barely afloat financial advisory business.

He doubts this way of living is sustainable.

It has been three weeks since The Slap. This is Rosario's affectionate term for the day Cecilia moved out. He is a mess of a man, but he maintains a good façade. He figures he will stay in town for a few weeks: the concept of a "for-good" separation seems so foreign to him. *Only losers get divorced.* Luckily, his neighbors Yana and Boris Goldenseal are more than happy to give Rosario a place to stay before he eventually moves back in with his mom for the majority of 2021.

Throughout their marriage, Cecilia and Rosario would often go to the Goldenseals' house for a friendly bonfire chat. They were the Fred and Ethel Mertz to their Ricky and Lucy Ricardo. Now, their house is his refuge, his classroom in the post-Slap school of life. It is here he begins to take seriously the study of how to not only be a good husband, but also how to be the man he was meant to be.

Rosario joins a sort of virtual AA group for men who have received The Slap in the form of divorces, affairs, and such. "The Bullet-proof Husband," it's called.

He logs into the Zoom call. There are a hundred and fifty men in attendance. It is silent apart from people logging in and their microphones picking up background noise before being muted by the moderators.

It begins. A man with a thick German accent welcomes every-one to the call.

"All right. Good evening, everybody. Welcome to our Thurs-day night question and answer session. As a reminder, please keep your cameras off to avoid distraction. We will start with submitted questions first and open it up to the floor afterward until a hard stop at eleven o'clock p.m. Eastern Standard Time."

About thirty minutes later, it is Rosario's turn. He introduces himself, and then the man with the German accent reads his submission.

"My wife of seven months left me about a month ago. We were supposed to move in with her dad after we sold the house, but now, she is not talking to me. I am staying at my friend's house until we can get back together."

There is a pause. Francis, one of the coaches (not the one with the German accent), asks, "So, what's your question?"

Rosario laughs because he notices Francis asks this a lot. Seems like some of these guys just need to vent, and it is at this moment he realizes he does, too.

But he doesn't vent: "I guess I don't have one. Just happy to be here."

"Rosario I'm glad to see you're on the call: some guys wait months before participating in these, so I'll give you props there. Unless you have a question, though, I'll let these guys drop their phone numbers in the chat and you can reach out to any of them to talk. You can see a few have already typed in their numbers for you. Let's go ahead to the next question. We have a lot tonight."

"Sure. Thanks, Francis."

Over the next year, Rosario will talk to hundreds of men from all over the world in various stages of their post-Slap lives. For the most part, these are successful men in their forties and fifties. Some of them are divorced. Those with kids are struggling but generally thriving when it comes to co-parenting. A beautifully large percentage have restored their marriages.

No, Rosario won't be among them.

SPANISH EXPLORERS

The weird adventures of the Spanish explorers aren't talked about in most schools, though nowadays, we are starting to understand how much of an unqualified ass Christopher Columbus was. Way before *La Nina, La Pinta, y La Santa Maria* set sail, hundreds of other explorers tried their hands at finding the new world. While of course, many of them died (the Crown apparently was willing to hand out ships to anyone who asked for one), many Spanish explorers would, after months at sea, eventually find land.

It was undoubtedly an exciting time when the lookout atop the mast would shout, *"Tierra!"* The crews would peek over the rails at their new home from afar, hoist the mainsails, yeet the calipers, knot the ladder sheets, and do whatever else the old-timey pirates would do to get the ship from sea to land. Eventually, they would make it, and as tradition dictated, they would stab a Spanish flag onto the beach and dedicate it to the Crown.

Months of hard work and searching at an end, you can just imagine the rejoicing and the partying that ensued. One can assume how, as soon as the rum was gone, they continued their exploration inland. Out came the machetes, carving up a trail through the thick forest of their new land. As they went, they encountered animals. The animals were much like the ones they remembered from Spain, but somehow more *exotic*, maybe because of how they moved or how they tasted. Those crewmembers who were knowledgeable of such things picked out plants to grind into spices, giving their exotic meals a familiar taste.

After a few days, up ahead in the distance, they spotted a village. They were surprised to find the natives quite technologically advanced. The buildings were not fancy but sturdy; the roads were not paved but also not just dirt. No problem, as the Spanish explorers were well prepared for any skirmishes that would arise with the locals.

The captain approached the first man he saw in the new land. Emotions were high as the pressure of this first contact became real. Would they be friendly? Were they cannibalistic? They seemed . . . *normal* . . .

"Greetings, local of these parts."

"How do you do?"

The crew gasped. Not only did the local speak the language of their captain, but he also had no noticeable accent. The captain maintains his composure.

"I see we are of the same language. Pray thee, what land is this?"

"España"

And the shouts of "*Godammit!*" reached the heavens.

Rosario asks for advice from his financial advisor/broker/best friend:

Dear Esmond,

I don't know what to do. I feel lost and depressed. I have hardly made any money in the last month, despite going on at least one appointment a day. These are supposed to be people with a minimum of 100,000 dollars ready to invest, but half are fakes and the other half I just can't get through to. Ever since Cecilia moved out, it feels like I've been fighting an uphill battle every day just to even see myself as a financial advisor. Any advice?

Rosario

Dear Rosario,

My man, it's okay. Don't forget that right now, you are dealing with something profoundly difficult. In fact, it's possibly the hardest thing a man can go through. It's perfectly okay for you to take some time away from the business and get things settled spiritually and emotionally before jumping back in.

Let's talk about that for a minute. You tell me you feel lost and depressed. Why is that? Is that because your wife left you?

I'm going to tell you this as a friend, specifically as a friend you gave permission to be a truth-teller in your life. Ask yourself this question, Rosario: what kind of role does Cecilia have in your life that she is allowed to depress and throw you off your mission? What kind of man would you be if you allowed someone (even your wife) to distract you from your God-given purpose in life? And once you figure that one out, answer me this: who holds the report card of your life? Is it Cecilia? Or is it your Heavenly Dad? Why are you letting anyone else besides your only True Guide tell you *anything* about yourself?

I don't have easy answers for you my friend, but don't think you can get back into your life work while ignoring your fundamental insecurities. You play for an audience of One, Rosario. He sees it all, and He always has your back.

Esmond

Next, he writes to Francis, the coach from The Bulletproof Husband who doesn't have a German accent:

Dear Francis,

Can you help me out here? Cecilia and I just had a bit of a kerfuffle. After I sold the house and moved back in with my mom, I rented out storage space for a few months. A few weeks ago, I emptied it out because I couldn't afford it anymore. I kept the valuable things in various friends' houses as well as my mom's house in Pennsylvania.

Now, I told Cecilia I was doing this. Before leaving New York, I gave her a key to the storage space so she could grab her things. Apparently, she told me to save her books or keep them safe or something, but I don't see that in any of our text conversations. It's possible she said it during a call, but we've literally talked on the phone two times in the last six months, so I don't think so. Anyway, now the storage unit is empty, and she is mad at me for not doing the one thing she asked. These books were incredibly valuable to her: high school yearbooks, stuff like that.

I feel terrible. Why is everything I do such a clusterfarse?

Rosario

Dear Rosario,

Let it all out, man. Have you had a bullet-pulling session over this? If not, here's your reminder.

Bullets are your suppressed pain, the insecurities that compromise your terms as a man. You need to get rid of these insecurities if you want to experience any level of healing. Now, you can't just talk about these issues. They are deep rooted.

Do you have jealousy issues with your wife? Good. Go to your private place and imagine her with some other man. A beautiful man, much better at everything than you. Imagine they're making love, and he is pleasuring her with a massive tool the way you never could. Release all the anger and jealousy by yelling, punching a pillow, whatever you need to do, until you are unbreakable.

If you feel you are a loser, it's not enough to talk to someone about it. You must get into a private space and release all the anger you feel about being a loser. Again, throw on Prince's "Purple Rain," call God a swear word—whatever it takes to release that emotion.

Once you have done this, only then can we get to the healing process. If it seems excessive and torturous, that's because it is. You know as well as anyone that if you feel deep down you are a loser, nothing anyone else says will change your mind. But if you can get to a point where feeling like a loser does not trigger you, nothing and no one will be able to use that against you. Eventually, nothing you or anyone else does will make you feel like a loser ever again.

Now, as for this situation about the storage unit, it reeks of the aforementioned "loser bullet." Remember: when your wife is upset, the things that come out of her mouth may or may not be accurate. It doesn't matter. Did she tell you to keep the books? Doesn't matter. Only a weak, insecure man would argue about whether she asked you to watch over the books.

Try to feel the *emotion* of what she is saying to you. She is really hurt that her books are gone. She might even know it's her fault, but she is hurt. And what do people do when they are hurt? They lash out. You are her husband. She is going to blame you for it. That's okay, you can take it. Hold your ground. It doesn't do you any good to argue, but it also doesn't help for you to grovel and say sorry. Remember, apologies are for when you do something that compromises your terms as a man. Whenever something like this happens, acknowledge what she's feeling and be there for her. "Gosh babe, I'm sorry this happened. I know they meant a lot to you; it must feel absolutely awful, losing these books that are so valuable. I love you." This is all you can do.

Cecilia doesn't need a weak man who tries to please her every time she stubs her toe. What she needs right now is a strong man who can listen to her vent, and if necessary, take a verbal beating. No matter what she says, you need to make her feel heard, understood, valued, and appreciated. You got this, brother.

Francis

Finally, he reaches out to the man he met from a Facebook ad and who became his long-time friend and mentor.

Dear Piers,

It's been a long time since I've thought about my "why." To tell you the truth, I've been avoiding thinking about it. In the last year, I've gone from financial advisor to sales development rep to account executive, and now, I'm an acquisitions manager with you. Under your tutelage, I've gotten eight houses under contract in less than two months.

Remember when we met, Piers? Five years ago, when we were selling those water purifiers over Facebook or something? It's been a crazy run, and I feel like with every recent change in my life, you've been there as my wise Yoda. Well, here we are, talking about my "why."

I did that "Seven-Layer Why" questionnaire you suggested: "I want *blank.*"

"Well, why do I want *blank?*"

"Because *blank* 2."

"Why is *blank* 2 important?"

And so on. If I'm honest with you (don't know what else I would be at this point), all I ended up with was, "Because I don't want to feel like a loser." But I don't really subscribe to that idea anymore.

I'm attaching the questionnaire for your review. Can you help challenge my thinking on this?

Rosario

Dear Rosario,

I do remember when we first met, will likely never forget. You would show up to each call motivated and ready to learn. Most guys would quit after not making a million dollars in a week. Then, once my company moved into real estate, you hopped in and became an invaluable asset, even doing an interview on a podcast. When you approached me to apply for the acquisitions manager position, I wasn't sure, but the team had a good feeling about you, and I can go to sleep feeling good about this decision to hire you.

After reviewing your Seven-Layer Why questionnaire, I think it would be helpful if I shared with you my vision for the company moving forward.

See, when we started buying houses in Kansas City, my idea was that we would build a world-class sales environment. You've heard me talk about this. Having you, Keith, and myself as the bedrock of our acquisitions team, we have produced some of the best months in the company's history. My dream was that within the year, we would expand the department to twelve to fifteen highly qualified, best-in-the-business salespeople, and I would promote the two of you to lead the charge in training and coaching.

Rosario, I don't think there is anything in your questionnaire that needs challenging. A man is confident in the mission God has placed inside of him. The questionnaire is designed to find that mission, not adjust it. Reading your questionnaire and thinking about your journey these last few years, I think there was a time in your life where you were motivated by money. This is a good thing for a salesperson. But after your wife left and you spent the year working on yourself, I'm starting to think that more than money, you were motivated by the desire to not be a loser. Again, not inherently a bad thing, but you must realize that all this emotional work you have done has made it impossible for you to fake your motivations. When I look at you now, I don't see a man haunted by insecurities.

So, here's the catch-22. All your life, you were able to be a good worker because you felt like if you didn't, then you were a loser. Now that you don't feel like a loser, you're either going to have to stop being a good worker, or you're going to have to find a new motivation.

What I'm really saying is this, Rosario: The reason you haven't come to this conclusion yourself is because you feel bad that after all the mentoring I've given you, you're going to quit working for me. Let me tell you right now, that is not the case. I told you about my vision for the company not to put pressure on you, but to show you the kind of person I am looking for as an acquisitions manager.

If, deep down, you are not motivated by building a world-class sales environment, then Rosario, you aren't doing me any favors by working with me on this. Why would I hire someone who hates their job when I know there is someone out there literally praying for this exact position? How could I ever find fault in your question-naire? You see, it is my great honor to help men find and pursue their life mission. If I am the one to finally help you find your talent again, this is the most fulfilling thing I can think of, worth more than a thousand properties.

Rosario, you are better at music than I'll ever be at real estate. If you need it, I give you permission to never make another phone call for me again. Just promise to do and be what God called you to do and be.

Love you, brother. Make me proud.

Piers

And so, it is July 18, 2021. The clock reads 3:07 p.m., and Rosario has just spent almost four hours on a video call with his longtime friend and mentor, Piers Noble. It has been another life-changing conversation that has led to a trajectory-redirecting decision.

He gets up from his desk and goes to the kitchen to make himself a late lunch.

After eating, he calls his friend Rich, owner of a music venue at Charlotte Beach.

"Guess I'm a musician again," says Rosario. "Let's go."

A few months later, Rosario looks down at the keys. He is the piano jockey on the newly inaugurated ship, the *CSS Radhames*. He begins the first few notes of Queen's "We Are The Champions" in C minor, the original key. Rosario has never been the best singer, but it makes him proud that he can sing a song in the same key as the legendary Freddie Mercury.

The crowd is a lot more diverse than he thought a cruise launching out of Long Beach, California, would be. There are young and old couples, there are families, there are so many single girls.

He gets to the chorus. Literally everyone sings along. He smiles, imagining they have been waiting for him all these years.

Not one of them have any idea that this recovering loser, this energy-rebate-specialist-turned-financial-advisor-turned-real estate investor is on his first day as a piano jockey. Like the Spanish explorers of old, Rosario had left his musical homeland looking for a new world, only to end up right back where he started—a little older and maybe, just maybe, a little wiser.

As he conducts the crowd to sing the last words of the song, a single tear wells up in his eye.

Applause.

CATALINA FOOL,
ENSENADA PROPHET

Off the coast of California is the small island of Catalina, known for being a popular cruise stop as well as having a museum dedicated to Wrigley gum.

It is a sleepy night at the Catalina police station. Detectives Rosa and Sabrasio are on the computers, filing in the usual tourist malfeasances. Police officer Goodman stands up to brew another pot of Folger's. Captain Hyatt sits in his office doing who-knows-what, his secretary Cristina playing Candy Crush on her cell phone. A standard, quiet weekday night at the Catalina police station.

All of a sudden, a commotion. Detectives Cruze and Petruzzi, along with a handful of other officers, bring in three men. All three are in their late twenties and soaked to the bone in seawater.

Detective Rosa looks up and sneers, "I'm not cleaning that up."

Petruzzi flashes an impetuous smile at Sabrasio. This'll be a real feather in his cap. Fourteen days earlier, someone issued a warrant out for these men's arrest. The young men have been caught trying to escape to the ferry as it went from the Catalina port back to mainland California. Now, he will get to the bottom of whatever they were guilty of.

Two of the men look eerily similar to each other. Young, handsome guys with big, friendly eyes, light skin, dark hair, shaved faces, and strong arms. Roughly five foot ten, the only thing distinguishing them is the accent: Sarel speaks with a charming South African accent while Carlos has a soft, western Mexican drawl.

The third man is about an inch shorter than the others. He is slightly tanner and plumper, also handsome, but with a left eye noticeably smaller than the right. Rosario stutters with a peculiarly nasal voice, hints of Puerto Rican slipping through the teeth.

After being processed into the system, they are ushered into the questioning room. A well-lit room with a table in the middle, Petruzzi sits on one side, facing the three men. They are calm but nervous.

Petruzzi begins.

"So, someone wanna tell me what's going on?"

Sarel and Carlos instinctively look at Rosario, who shrugs.

"Okay, guess I'll start," he says with a bashful smile. "It began innocently enough. Sarel and I worked together on the cruise ship *CSS Radhames*. I was a piano jockey and he worked in the art gallery. We were good friends from the start, but we could never hang outside the ship because Sarel had to work all the time."

"And what, didn't you have to work?"

Sarel laughs at this and butts in: "No way! He's the piano man! Rosario only works like three or four hours a night, six nights a week, so he gets off the ship every time it ports. I was actually starting to get a little jealous, to be honest. But right as the thought entered my mind, Rosario comes up with the craziest idea. He comes back to the ship one day and says, 'Hey, Sarel, I just met a guy in Ensenada who looks *just* like you. Same face, same voice, everything.'"

Petruzzi can only assume he means Carlos. Turning to him, he asks, "And that was you?"

"*Sí, señor*. Well, minus the voice," laughs Carlos. "Rosario would come into the resort like clockwork where I worked twice a week on Sundays and Wednesdays, because those were the days that the cruise ship *CSS Radhames* came to port in my hometown of Ensenada, Baja California. The first day we meet he tells me he knows a guy on the ship who looks like me. We start chatting and I suppose I say something like, 'Oh man, Rosario. I would love to work on a cruise ship. How crazy would it be if me and your friend traded places just for a few days?' And thus, it all started." Carlos looks down at his cuffed hands. He frowns. "I guess this is all my fault, isn't it?"

After a solemn moment, Rosario breaks out a goose honk of a laugh. "Damn, Carlos, way to give up the fight! You're really gonna tell them you're guilty already?"

Petruzzi shoots him a disapproving look; Rosario retracts.

"Now, don't get me wrong, sir," says Rosario. "I'm not a 'think-of-others-first' or 'go-out of-my-way-for-someone-else' kind of guy, but I like Sarel. He's a great guy, and he deserved a break from the ship's art gallery. So, I'm thinking, *How could we make this happen?*"

Sarel butts in. "Initially, I'm thinking this is a terrible idea and we shouldn't even entertain it. But honestly, Rosario kept bringing it up, and every week, he would show me pictures and videos of himself partying with some bikinis. Eventually, we figure out a plan. I give Rosario my training manual for working at an art gallery, and the next port day in Ensenada, he gives it to Carlos, who plans to study it for a week before coming onto the ship. But just for three days."

Petruzzi takes notes while also taking in this ridiculous sitcom. These are not criminals, obviously, though the switcheroo they're describing does have some serious visa implications. "So, you're telling me that Carlos just learned how to be an art gallery worker over the course of a week, and everyone bought that?"

Carlos and Sarel look at each other and after a pause, give a nod. Rosario snorts, "What, like it's hard?"

At this point, Sarel loses his cool for a moment. "Wish you would take this a tad more serious, piano man! Don't you know what's at stake here?"

Rosario drops a blank look. "Not really." He turns to Petruzzi. "What is at stake here?"

"Let's just have you guys finish the story. Then we can talk about what's at stake."

A moment of tension passes.

"Okay," continues Petruzzi. "So Sarel is off the ship, Carlos has taken over the art gallery, and no one suspects anything. How did the three of you end up in Catalina?"

The men sit there awkwardly, trying to figure out how to tell the rest of the story. Eventually, Rosario continues.

"So, two things happened simultaneously. Things were going well for a month or so. It's a lovely system we came up with: every Wednesday, Sarel got off the ship and Carlos got on. Every Sunday, Carlos got off and Sarel got on. Sarel was really enjoying having some days off the boat and Carlos was killing it in the art gallery. The paycheck was split fifty-fifty—everybody wins.

"One day, Sarel decides he doesn't want to just see Ensenada, so he takes a speedboat out to Catalina. This is fine, because Carlos can just stay onboard for another couple of days and swap out at Catalina instead of Ensenada.

"This seems like a good idea to Carlos too, because now he'll be able to check out Catalina as well, so we make another switch." He turns to Carlos. "Why don't you take over on what happens next?"

Sarel runs his fingers across the table. "Oh, real smooth, Ros."

"What?"

"Guys, it's fine." Carlos attempts to keep the peace. "I'll go."

Sarel turns away from Carlos and Rosario.

"When I first got off in Catalina," began Carlos, "I noticed this lovely vacant storefront right there on Green Pleasure Pier. As Rosario and I walked around talking with some of the locals, we learned it used to be an ice cream shop and was actually still owned by this nice old couple in one of the mountaintop mansions on the island. But after their daughter died a year before, they closed up and now the only ice cream place in town was a Coldstone Creamery."

"Oh yeah, I remember that place," Petruzzi contributed. "Jamey-O's. Didn't realize that's what happened."

"Sure, sure," says Carlos. "Anyways, I tell Rosario about my grandmother back in Mexico who had this recipe for sugar-free ice cream, and once again my fat tongue gets me in trouble. I say aloud something like, 'I bet the people of Catalina would love a sugar-free ice cream place,' then before I know it, Rosario has convinced me to go with him and visit this old couple."

Petruzzi raises an eyebrow. This Rosario guy is a hell of an instigator. Almost as if he could read his thoughts, Rosario flashes a big-toothed smile at the detective.

"And that was pretty much it. We convince the old couple to let us use their spot to sell my grandmother's sugar-free ice cream. I spend the next several days getting materials and machines for the shop, and within the week, we're in business."

"And I was against it the whole time!" declares Sarel. "You think I wanted to get off the boat so I could work an ice cream shop?"

Now it is Carlos's turn to raise his voice. "Whatever, man! You could have stayed on the boat at this point for all I cared—I loved working that place!"

Rosario laughs. "Bitch, who you fooling? Every week you couldn't wait to get off the boat. Besides," he explains to Petruzzi, "both his art gallery and my piano bar contract ended about a month ago, so all three of us have been living here on your beautiful island ever since."

Sarel leans back in his chair.

Turning back to Petruzzi, Carlos continues, "But before their contracts finished, and when we were going in and out of Catalina and not Ensenada, we got to know the people pretty well. They loved our newly revamped storefront. Turns out an island full of rich, old people really appreciate a diabetic-friendly dessert stop, and over time, we had so much business we had to hire kids to keep up with the crowds!"

At this point, Petruzzi has no idea where this story is going. Clearly, what these guys are doing is illegal, but it is so charming, he kind of wishes he didn't have to be a cop right now.

"I see that smile, sir," says Rosario.

Petruzzi regains his posture. "Please continue."

Sarel takes over. "I mean, you know what happened next, sir. Eventually, your town officials started coming in on a weekly basis, asking questions. Taxes, permits, visas, licenses, et cetera. We tried brushing them off, stalling. Luckily, we were usually pretty busy when they came in, so that helped. Eventually, they put out a warrant, your men came in, and we tried to escape on the ferry. Now, we await the swift hand of justice on her journey to . . ."

But before Sarel can finish this overly poetic stave, there is a clamor outside. Old hands pound on the glass of the questioning room door. Detectives Rosa and Sabrasio barge in and struggle to keep the door shut behind them.

"Petruzzi, who are these guys?" pants Sabrasio. "We've got over fifty old people in the station demanding to see you, saying something about 'leave the Jamey-O boys alone' and making a mess."

Sabrasio gives him a stern look. "I swear to God, Petruzzi. This better not take all night. *Dancing with the Stars* starts at nine o'clock."

At this, Petruzzi shakes his head in confusion. He gets up, signaling for the three men to stay seated while he deals with the mob. He opens the door and heads out.

In the main office area, he wades through the people while trying to calm them down. Eventually, he gets everyone quiet. He takes a deep breath.

"Thank you. Now, how can I help you all?"

"Sweetie, you need to let these boys go," says an old lady, stepping forward. She is supported by a cane and sports the latest in purple flowered sleepwear.

Petruzzi's eyes widen. "*Grandma?*"

"You listen here, Jakey. These boys have opened up the finest dessert establishment this island has ever seen. Do you understand I haven't eaten anything sweet in twenty years because of my diabetes? Look at Barb! She hasn't had sugar since Desert Storm! I swear to you, Jakey, if you take away our sugar-free ice cream, we will tear this police station down!"

"Grandma, you know I have to send these guys mainland. What they're doing is wrong. Two of them are working in the country without visas, and they are employing teenagers illegally."

Another old man chimes in: "You think we care about any of that stuff, son? What, it's all a matter of money isn't it?"

"I mean, yeah, it is but—"

"Then let *us* pay it, for God's sake."

"It's not that easy, it's—"

"Jakey, come here." Detective Petruzzi's grandma beckons him over to her. As he approaches, she says, "Closer."

He bends his ear down to her face.

"If you send these boys mainland" she whispers, "I'm going to shove my cane up your bootyhole."

"Gah!" Petruzzi jumps back. "Okay, okay, okay! Everyone, calm down. Good God, what is going on here? You all are really willing to pay all the business expenses of this place?"

Another wiser, less manic voice answers, "I mean, not forever, Jake. But entrepreneurship is tough these days. These are three very wise, very talented young men who have brought a wonderful gift to the people of Catalina. Don't take that away from them because they did it wrong the first time. Let us help them out."

And so, Detective Petruzzi gives the orders to uncuff Sarel, Rosario, and Carlos. That night, the respective authorities are contacted with the news that the owners of the illicit ice cream shop known as Jamey-O's have been apprehended. The following day is spent filling out paperwork and collecting money from the fifty-one people who stormed the police station the previous night. All together, they raise twenty-four thousand dollars for taxes, permits, visas, and licenses.

By noon of the day after that, Jamey-O's is back in business, and they even set up a piano bar for Rosario to entertain the locals on Friday nights.

Don't even think about taking away the people's ice cream.

AN ECCENTRIC TIME TRAVELER

-one-

The progression of social equality over the timeline of the human race is a fascinating one, and it may surprise you to realize how the entirety of the spectrum was covered in only one thousand years.

Starting in the 19th and 20th centuries, the idea was introduced that people other than white men had voices and needed to be heard. Female writers shared their experiences, bringing color to the bland, male-dominated perspectives and worldviews. The US Civil Rights movement saw the black man standing up and demanding equal treatment. Nothing more than lip service, of course, until the election of the first black man as President of the United States in the 2008th year.

Barack Obama, the forty-fourth man elected to that office, did by no means see the end of racism in his lifetime, as even

in my time it exists as an annoying parasite. Regardless, for several years after his tenure, many Americans looked upon Barack Obama as a hero, launching a long line of diverse leaders. The 21st century saw Latinas taking over as CEOs; it saw the LGBT+ community leading breakthroughs in science. Companies began to incorporate equal opportunity in their training manuals. Even the US military, long known to be the most stubborn single-faced conglomerate, saw both cis and transgender soldiers fighting and dying together on the fields. Fifty years after Obama, the country elected Billie Eilish as its first female president. Extraordinary leaps and bounds happened within this century, marking it the Golden Age of social equality.

Of course, there were issues along the way. Many times, other urgencies placed themselves on the front page of newspapers, and it was in these times the priority of social equality found itself challenged. Would the country return to "letting the men handle things," or would they add "listening to everyone's opinions" to the day's agenda?

> *The decision to place social equality as a head*
> *priority cannot allow for periods of apathy.*
> *—Joe Biden*

For the most part, the early leaders of the 21st century stood their ground, though maintaining the forward progress was at times impossibly difficult. For instance, when Joe Biden took the Presidency in the 2020th year, he found himself dealing with a pandemic of cosmic proportions. His people were dying left and right. Other countries such as New Zealand and Scandinavia had obliterated the pandemic from their borders. (No surprise to anyone: their leadership was primarily female.) But Biden's country, which was fighting hard against the progression, could not seem to deal with the pandemic in any meaningful way.

While most would get frustrated to the point of militarization, Biden turned the tables. He knew the physical pandemic would someday end. Nevertheless, if every time a rough situation showed up, the nation returned to the old ways of the white man making decisions for everyone, they would never have a unified society. Thus, he chose to listen, to surround himself with people of all races, creeds, abilities, and orientations. For the larger part of his appointment, many criticized Joe Biden for not getting anything done, but the precedent he set would tear down the walls for years to come.

The pandemic came to a close toward the end of his presidency. It had claimed close to one million lives worldwide. Thanks to Biden's decisive actions, it did not claim the end of social equality.

So continued the 21st-century march toward progress. It was a remarkable time in the trajectory of the human race. Subsequent generations have looked back at many of the medical and technological advancements of the era as foundational to their own societies, and though there are far too many to choose from, it is widely held that The Institution of Sign Language Education was the pivotal point in this progression.

Under the leadership of first female president Billie Eilish in the 2064th year, The Institution of Sign Language Education became both a national requirement and an unexpected success. While the nation had its share of complaints, within two generations, the entirety of the population was fluent. Naturally, it began with the teaching of the children. After about twenty years, articulacy was required in order to access employment at various high-level workplaces. Another five years witnessed the last family-owned sushi restaurants requiring it among their handful of employees.

Small but loud, the critics of this requirement questioned the need for learning to sign, as the population of deaf and hard-of-hearing was "hardly worth the effort, and they only hang out with each other, anyway."

The election of the first deaf president, Andrew Magnuson, in the 2116th year once and for all silenced the argument. He posited that the reason the deaf and hard-of-hearing community isolated themselves was due to the lack of sensitivity the hearing community had shown them. But now, thanks to the courage and foresight of Billie Eilish, every person had deaf friends. As a result, when Magnuson moved to make American Sign Language the official language of the United States, it was a landslide victory in every deciding congress of the country.

With the rise of the new national dialect, other countries followed suit. Within one hundred years of Billie Eilish's Institution, international companies moved to making signing their official language, and English of course remained the primary spoken form of communication for benefit of the visually impaired. Not since before the Tower of Babel had something of this stature been achieved. The world had finally come together in one tongue, a newly developed International Sign Language.

-two-

At this point, I feel it necessary to introduce myself.

My name is Henri Poisser. I am—technically—thirty-seven years old and was born in the year 3001. By profession, I am a time traveler. The current year from my perspective is 3038.

I have been among you, people of the 21st century. I have been among the apes as well. In my time and among my people, some still debate which species deserves to be at the top. No doubt it will come as a surprise to you, my 21st-century readers, when I say that within a thousand years, Earth will indeed be ruled by apes.

You will forgive opening with a chapter on social equality, but I felt I had to preface my account with a brief history of the events that led to the current state my people find themselves in. The cleverest among you will have already concluded the next series of events within this progression, and before going any further, it is important that you understand the complexity of the issue.

I and those with me believe in the brotherhood of humanity. We believe in a world that lives together in harmony. Of course, there are those who would corrupt the purity of our intention and blame change for any problems that arise. My hope is that I can bring clarity to the issues.

You see, society has continued to strive in science and progress, but there are groups that have perpetually struggled to accept the reality of a human and ape coexistence. It is for this reason that in the year of my writing, the SAPLH (Society for the Advancement of People with Less Hair) is entrenched in a confusing battle with no one, in a world where the only thing not tolerated is intolerance. There are those who blame the apes for the issues that are forcing me to write my story. I am not among their number, but mine is a unique stance.

The conversation is a hard one to articulate. You can likely see this by the difficulty I have in merely talking about it. The initial problem about our situation is that the apes are, in a word, *nice*. They have compromised our government largely due to the fact that they are extremely understanding of humans. It all happened so slowly and subtly that it almost looks natural; many would argue it *is* the natural evolution of society. Maybe I am wrong. Maybe it is all paranoia and I am just an eccentric time traveler. Still, I and those with me cannot shake the feeling that *something* is wrong.

I hope you will start to see a fragment of my mind about our situation. But before discussing further the issue at hand, I shall return to the history of social equality to clarify how things got to their current state.

-three-

Teaching sign language to the apes was not a new idea. From the start of the 21st century, videos floated around the internet of real conversations between humans and apes, conversing mostly about how the humans were tearing down the apes' habitat. This was used to garner support for environmental preservation, and many people thought nothing of it. It is doubtful anyone would have assumed any interspecies learning was occurring beside the obvious and necessary sensitivity toward protecting the jungles.

Note: the reality of the phenomenon of the apes adopting sign language is just as with the teaching of children. Learning to communicate does not occur in a vacuum. Through new words, the learner absorbs new concepts. Visualize an ape learning the word "jealousy" for the first time. The teacher puts her pinky finger to the side of her lip and flicks down. Now, the ape will now know how to sign that one word. But it will take hundreds of words to illustrate the *idea* of jealousy, which is the inevitable next step. Jealousy is not a primary emotion for the natural ape, but now his head is filled with questions: *Why does he have a banana and I don't? Why did she mate with him and not me?* Consequently, to teach sign language to an ape is, in a way, to teach him to be human. Emotions, ethics, values, beliefs, are instilled in the apes via this shared language.

It was not long before apes grew into a subculture of society. In the 2231st year, history was made when a group of four brave, young apes made the decision to attend human school for the first time. Two of them dropped out after the first year, but Jarif the orangutan and Herschon the gorilla succeeded in being the first apes to complete all twelve years of human public school. The precedent was now set; by the end of the year 2256, apes accounted for a stunning 2.1 percent of students matriculated in the United States public school system.

Sparing all tedious detail, over time, the apes began participating in practically every part of human society. They took roles as janitors all the way to high-level executive positions. The majority of people were so enamored with this progression, they could see no problem with it. The inclusion of another species was seen as something to be celebrated, not questioned.

Opponents of this progression were frustrated in a similar way to the opponents of women's rights in the 20th century. History reminds us that within a few years of girls being allowed to go to school with boys, studies came out showing that female test score averages were noticeably higher. In the same way, shortly after their inclusion into the public schools, the average ape test scores began to overtake those of the humans.

And so it came to pass that apes not only entered human society, but also thrived in almost every arena of it. From the workplace to religious organizations, from design and construction to sports and journalism, from science and medicine to politics, it was nothing out of the ordinary to have apes as coworkers or even as bosses.

It has now been six hundred years since the first ape was elected president in 2438. His name was Rypi Borzill. This was not done as a joke; he was elected in the same manner as every other president in the history of America. He campaigned, he fundraised, and his platform was nothing new or controversial. President Borzill was just a silverback gorilla who wore a suit and had the charisma and leadership required for the position. For the preceding eight years, in fact, he had represented the good people of Hanover, Connecticut, and its outlying areas as a senator.

Thus, the solo reign of the human being reached its end: the ape had risen to walk hand-in-hand next to us.

-four-

I look back in wonder at the slow, steady transition of power from man to ape. You will forgive my heresy of comparison, my

21st-century readers, but I cannot help but think of the Nazis. It took less than forty years for a German dictator to instill across his citizenry a new way of living and thinking. A massive shift, from peace-loving, happy yodelers to apathetic killers. In only forty years!

In truth, compared to the cultural shift that drives my vendetta, every other shift in any culture in the history of earth is a childishly hasty one. It was over the patient course of more than a thousand years the apes waited to spring their shift upon the human race. And yet, it really wasn't "sprung" by any definition of the word, was it?

You will likely be wondering what it is that is forcing me to write such a critique of the times.

So far, things sound relatively harmless, no?

You might be thinking the apes established a strange banana-based diet to control us with or began permitting humans to be kept as pets. Maybe they have been using us for science experiments, the way we sent monkeys into space in the 1960s. Perhaps through crossbreeding, ridiculous human-ape mixes are a disgusting affront to life as God intended (yes, by the way, human-ape hybrids do exist).

But it is none of these things.

No, the shift has been a subtle one, hidden by centuries of celebrating the progress of equality.

It is a shift no one could even be said to take the blame for, as it took nearly a thousand years for anyone to even notice. A shift only recently acknowledged for the first time.

Actually, in my time, it was just a few days ago.

To your 21st-century minds, it will strike you as so incomprehensible you might not believe it, yet as sure as my name is Henri Poisser, it is the truth.

Once you understand the world that I live in, you will understand why the SAPLH began to commission time travelers to right this situation at the root.

The shift was first articulated in the form of one question, asked by an older member of the board of directors, stirring the frenzy we had been waiting almost a decade for.

Rickren y'Stadvenjanesol had been one of the founding fathers of the SAPLH, along with his sister, Yulia, a mechanic named Thiless Jurjong, a senator named Wik Raymenkris, and a schoolteacher named Lucia Maimazer. They organized and held the first meeting of the Society for the Advancement of People with No Hair in September of year 3029, before changing it to "Little Hair" to accommodate the aforementioned "affronts to life as God intended." We are a self-admittedly hard-to-pin-down bunch, motivated primarily by the feeling that *something* is wrong.

The founders were hardly the first to feel this way, as Rickren was quick to remind people, and the purpose of the group was not to stir up undue hatred toward the apes. It was more a support group for any person struggling with the coexistence of man and ape. Not exactly the greatest idea for a group, yet it burned like an ember in so many people's minds that it couldn't help but catch on.

Meetings initially were held in the basement of a church in Birmingham, Alabama. We disguised it by calling ourselves Alcoholics Anonymous, and in the nine years following the inauguration of the SAPLH, we regrettably accomplished little due to the solvent nature of our mission. To be fair, the ape-led government allowed us a voice and a small bit of funding. However, without a unified stance, we were seen as little more than a Boys & Girls Club.

It was a muggy April 16th, 3038. This was the night Rickren asked the question that would solidify the SAPLH's true mission. We had actually begun discussing whether disbanding the group would be in the best interests of all involved. One can hardly imagine the mind-numbingly uninspired nature of these meetings, discussing at lengths our sense that something was out of place. Without a leading concept, it is a miracle we lasted the nine years without putting a finger on the issue.

But consider, my friends, the boiling point of water.

At ninety-seven degrees Celsius, nothing happens. Ninety-eight degrees, nothing. Even at ninety-nine degrees Celsius, the water is hot but you see no motion within.

Finally, give it that hundredth degree, and the fireworks begin.

As we were concluding the meeting on April 16, 3038, it felt likely to be one of the last, if not *the* last gathering of the SAPLH. It had been another hour in a long line of directionless banter.

But picture this: as people are putting away chairs and clearing the area, a large stack of chairs tips over and initiates a domino effect with nearby stacks, creating a mass cacophony magnified by the gym's glorious acoustics. There is a moment of silence, then a howl of "*Nooo!*"

Jylt Lopduug, a younger member, points out that the chairs fell in a pattern resembling a flaccid penis. An unexpected installation of modern art.

This provokes much laughter, and cheers all around.

As they get back to restacking, Rickren turns to his sister and says, "You know, I just thought of something: *When was the last time a new work of art was created?*"

THE PLANET OF THE APES CONCERTO

-one-

When was the last time a new work of art was created?

I, Henri Poisser, could not begin to tell you how much this question affected the SAPLH. None of us had ever experienced new art ourselves. The most recent work was created nearly four hundred years ago, and we'd never thought much of it.

And so, the flaccid-penis chair installation stirred something deep within all of us.

Upon undertaking my own research to discover what happened to the arts in this ape-dominated planet, I discovered something striking. This involves you, my 21st-century readers, for it so happens that the death of art had been a topic talked about for generations.

Throughout your time, musicians were convinced elitism would lead to the end of art. This was an argument largely centered around the audience's experience, this idea that people had little to no attention for new music, that all they wanted was something "with a beat" and God help it if it did not have lyrics. No one ever considered the death of art would come from a lack of motivation of the creators themselves. Take for instance, this episode in the annals of 19th-century composition:

A crisis hit the center of the music world in the year 1827, after the death of Ludwig van Beethoven. After his great work, his swan song, his "Ode To Joy," people were convinced we had reached the end of music.

"What else is to be said?" wrote a shy, young Franz Schubert. "The master has said it all; he has closed the book on orchestral music with his death."

This attitude was not unique to him. For years, original composition was at a standstill. All new works were held up against the legacy of Ludwig van Beethoven and consistently found wanting. It wasn't until Johannes Brahms premiered his first symphony in 1876 that it could be said a creative spirit had resurged in the world.

In 2669, the last work by composer Gerald B. Giner premiered. It was a groundbreaking work, his *Unity Finale*. A glorious piece of music with something for everyone. More popular even than any song released by the late, great President Billie Eilish. This time however, after Giner's death four years later, the conversations around the future of music did not percolate. You see, though it was a trying time for composers after Beethoven's death in the 19th century, there was still the effort. Though they were generally pessimistic, people still took the step of *discussing* what would follow. This made all the difference. But now that the last great composer was gone, the 27th century saw a different response: none at all.

Over time, the subject of music and art was reserved for studying the classics. No one thought anything of it; we all just assumed this was the way things were. For fifty years after Gerald B. Giner's death, did musicians continue to perform? Of course, what else were they to do?

It is just that none of it was new.

Without new works to perform or even critique, musicians lost the sense of purpose to do their work. Giner's music again begged the question, "What else is to be said?"

This time, no Brahms took up the mantle.

–two–

"How is this even possible?" asks Rickren amid the frantic chatter.

"For some reason, after the apes take over, eventually, new art just stops happening."

"So, it *is* their fault!"

"Well, I wouldn't go that far. They didn't actually tell us to stop making art."

"No, but you didn't see them contributing anything."

"I thought I remember reading something about apes making sculptures in school?"

"No, no, that was the elephants—"

"Maybe it was the elephants' fault."

"Can we stay on topic?"

Ad nauseum.

After much heated discussion, the newly revitalized SAPLH decides to commission three time travelers to attempt to fix the issue of no new art. We are to come up with and present to the board a plan for how best to achieve this goal: to inspire 27th-century musicians to take up Giner's mantle after his death.

The next day, the other two time travelers and I meet to discuss strategy. Hvensel and Grun are two of the finest travelers I know. We have gone on several missions together; this is a stimulating reunion we are each grateful for. After some initial pleasantries, we begin to plan our approach.

Hvensel feels if we are to have any effect within the great social progression that led to the rule of the ape, fear is our best weapon. It is through suffering, he argues, that great art is created. He gives the example of masters Gustav Mahler and Sergei Prokofiev, who wrote some of the most beautiful music in dangerous times under horrid regimes. Hvensel explains how it was the fear they felt for their own lives as well as the lives of their families that inspired the *Resurrection Symphony* and *Love for Three Oranges*. And where would George Rochberg's *Ricordanza* be without the death of his daughter to spur him on?

In horror, I ask what he intended to do to scare the 27th-century musicians into creation. Fortunately, he has no idea.

I personally have a difficult time justifying Hvensel's logic. As convinced as he is, we all innately understand none of us have a clue of how the artist mind works; none of us know how to play an instrument. None of us have ever even drawn a picture.

We sit there for several moments in silence.

How far humanity has come.

Many ideas are tossed around, as brainstorming goes. Eventually, it is Grun's idea to go back to the year 1968 and create a dramatic series of films, aptly titled *The Planet of the Apes*. My 21st-century readers will likely have seen some or all of this franchise, at which point you might be struggling to justify the tale I have told with the tale shown in the movies.

This is Hvensel and Grun's fear-based reasoning in a nutshell: if they can plant inside the collective subconscious the idea that a planet ruled by apes will lead to a tyrannical oppression of humans, then they will think twice about teaching the apes sign language and incorporating them into society. The fear of what *might* happen will keep *anything* from happening.

Naturally, I feel this is not going to work. Nevertheless, Hvensel and Grun are set on instilling fear in the humans. Since I want no part in this, we make the difficult decision to part ways.

When we approach the board of the SAPLH the next day, they are not in the least bit thrilled to learn of our schism. It is difficult for me to articulate my concern, particularly because I have no idea of my own to present. Thus, I am taken off the mission entirely.

Hvensel and Grun pack their things and prepare for their long voyage.

-three-

A NOTE ON TIME TRAVEL

The complex science of time travel received its fair share of misunderstandings when it was discovered, invented, and perfected in the mid-30th century. This was of course due to the foolish assumptions made in such ancient works as Ray Bradbury's A Sound of Thunder *and the 1989 cult classic film* Bill and Ted's Excellent Adventure.

For as long as men had it in mind, they assumed that something called "the butterfly effect" was a dominating force in the universe. In reality, there is no such thing. Stepping on a butterfly in Jurassic times will not bring about a catastrophic end to humanity seventy million years later. You also cannot leave keys on a table so your future self will remember you did so. Meeting your parents before they meet each other and stifling their plans to make love and produce you will not result in your deletion.

However, convincing your pre-wed parents to force their future son to study piano can affect the future. Why? It comes down to the difference between the Abstract and the Physical. Anything of a physical nature that happens throughout history is set in stone. The butterfly is, in a sense, indestructible until the moment it is destined to fall. The car keys, if they are destined to be hiding in a glove compartment, will stay there no matter how many times you go back and put them on the table. The birth of a human is a physical act: your corporeal existence, therefore, is set in stone.

On the other hand, abstract forces, such as ideas and emotions, are not set in stone. You can, for instance, go back in time and convince your young self to take his piano studies seriously. When you return to your own time, you will implant in yourself however many years of expertise to find you are now a world-renowned keyboard virtuoso.

This may seem a convenient loophole, my 21st-century readers; trust me when I say it hardly classifies. Following the odd continuity within the inner workings of time travel, new physical events are possible: that is, you cannot trifle with your own existence, but you can come back to discover that your parents had another baby.

At this point, the question of memory becomes tricky; you will suddenly have years of recollections growing up with your little sister. You will also remember not growing up with your little sister.

It is a lonely struggle, as it is exclusively the time travelers themselves who are affected. Yes, there are always those involved with the time traveler's journey. For instance, the people they go back in time to meet or, if applicable, whoever commissions them. These people exist in a quantum memory limbo, where they see the effects of the time traveler's mission, but they themselves do not get new memories implanted like the time travelers do. An unfortunate side effect of this implantation is that oftentimes, a time traveler will go mad after undergoing too many missions. This is the sacrifice a mind must make if it attempts to justify too many realities.

-four-

"Henri, do you have any other ideas?"

"You mean, any ideas at all?"

I am mostly just relieved to discover Hvensel and Grun's *Planet of the Apes* idea has failed. The SAPLH is not angry, just disappointed. They have spent all of the year's budget on sending the two time travelers back to the 20th century, and all for nothing. No implanted memories, no change of leadership, and most upsettingly, no new art.

Events go by fast when you're dealing with time travel. Rickren presented the fateful question on a Monday night. Tuesday, we were commissioned. Wednesday, we came up with a plan. Thursday, the travelers left without me; I ate mozzarella sticks. Friday, they returned with a failed mission report.

Saturday comes, and the SAPLH is asking me to go on a solo mission with hardly a third of the resources they gave Hvensel and Grun.

"We'd love to be able to pay you more, Henri. But we can't, it's all gone. And even if we did have money, we have to be reasonable. It's not like you're going back there with a better idea."

"Wow. Subtle."

Then it hit me.

"*Subtle.*"

"Yes, we heard you the first time, Henri."

"No, no, no, no," I said. "I have my idea. Get the machine fueled up, I'm ready."

Admittedly, it was a complicated idea. I wasn't quite sure it would work. But I told them my logic.

"The nature of great art is subtlety, ambiguity. What is universal can never be singular. In the music world, they have things like diminished dominant chords that, according to common practice rules of harmony, act as musical wild cards. Any diminished dominant chord can go to one of *eight* different tonalities. Composers had a field day with this when they discovered it. Meanwhile, songs like Queen's "Bohemian Rhapsody" and Toto's "Africa" make no sense lyrically and utilize both erratic and popular progressions—and people love it.

"Our mission is to inspire the 27th-century musicians to create, but that doesn't just happen because someone tells them to. Inspiration comes out through involuntary means in prepared vessels. Hvensel and Grun tried to force a reaction out of humanity, tried to force on people an irrational fear of apes. I'm not going to do that. I'm going to prepare the vessel."

Blank stares all across the room.

"Okay, Henri. Whatever you say."

Sunday comes.

I get in the machine.

No one even attends the launch. Hvensel and Grun got a whole party. I got Rickren and Yulia y'Stadvenjanesol waving me goodbye.

Sigh.

-five-

My journey begins in turn-of-the-century Germany. The year is 1799. Beethoven is currently working on his magnificent *Violin Sonata in C Minor*.

I immediately break the first rule of time travel: I tell Beethoven everything. I tell him about my mission. I tell him about the social equality movement. I tell him about the incorporation of the apes. I tell him about Gerald B. Giner and the death of art itself.

Most problematically, I tell him about his impact on literally every other artist to come after him.

(I choose not to tell him that within ten years he will lose all hearing ability, but I do suggest learning sign language.)

Surprisingly—or perhaps unsurprisingly—he is a great listener through it all.

"You say there is no artist to come who will not be influenced by my work?"

"Not a one."

"I refuse to believe that, Mr. Henri Poisser. You must go and find them, the artist unaffected, for if I am to write a great work to protect the future of my species, I will need *that* person's help."

To be sent on a centuries-long hunt for an "artist unaffected" is not what I was expecting, but I eagerly take to it. This is a unique opportunity to meet some of my favorites at their peak creativity.

In 1973, I visit the legendary Stevland Morris, or as you may know him, Stevie Wonder. He is having lunch at Carmine's in New York

City. We talk about his upcoming album, *Innervisions*. I am in the middle of telling him how I bet the album will rescue pop music from the white-dominated industry when he spills his maracuja soda all over my lap.

"Oh Henri, I'm so sorry, brother."

"Don't you worry 'bout a thing, Stevie."

He stares at me with those blind eyes behind dark shades.

"Funny. That's the name of one of the songs on the album."

"You don't say? What inspired you to write that? And while we're at it, tell me about some of your overall musical influences."

Wouldn't you believe it? The first name out of Stevie's mouth is Beethoven.

In 1910, I visit Igor Stravinsky after the premiere of his *Firebird* ballet, a VIP event at Diaghilev's lakeside mansion outside Paris.

"Incredible, powerful, an absolute miracle, absolute honor to be here at the premiere, Mr. Stravinsky."

"Thank you for your kind words, Mr. Poisser. I can only hope for such a great reception for my next work, *Le Sacre du Printemps*, but only time will tell. Did you have a favorite moment this evening?"

"Oh, my goodness, I nearly jumped out of my seat at the orchestral hits in the Kaohlcel's "Dans Infernal"! Would not surprise me one bit if seventy years from now, those hits become standard material sampled in American dance music."

"Indeed, a composer can ask for no greater flattery than to be robbed in this manner."

"Cheers to that, Mr. Stravinsky. Curious subject, robbery. Any particular composers you find yourself stealing from?"

Again, the unescapable influence of Beethoven seeps in. To Russia of all places!

My search seems fruitless for so long, my 21st-century reader. A similar conversation happens with Richard Wagner during his *Der Ring des Nibelungen* hiatus, in between the success of *Tristan und Isolde* and the first performance of *Die Meistersinger von Nurnberg* in the Bayreuth Opera House.

After this, I attempt to reach out to artists in other mediums. I go to see the groundbreaking Martha Graham in 1935 performing *Frontiers* for a diverse crowd of students, politicians, homosexuals, and other dancers. In 1913, I catch Oscar Kokoschka for an afternoon riverside walk and he shows me the studio where he just added the finishing touches to his *Bride of the Wind*. I even meet Auguste Rodin in 1915 outside of his chiropractor's office. It turns out, on top of having to comprehend Rainer Maria Rilke's writing about his work, he also has chronic back pain.

Everywhere I go, artists in all mediums pointing to Ludwig van Beethoven as a prominent mentor for their own expression: *The first romantic! The first composer to take off the wig! He put a choir in the "Ode to Joy"! He wrote music while completely unable to hear it! He goes from G major to B major with no transition! He pays tribute to the Ottomans, his enemies, by using a Turkish march to accompany the same melody with which he calls brothers to live together in harmony!*

His heart and soul, his very being, is a calling forth of the salvation we all seek in our meager human condition!

And on the list goes. A tad overbearing if you ask me.

My next stop is Andé, France in 1964. I have never even heard Henri Dutilleux's music, but a young pianist studying at the Moscow Conservatory recommends I pay him a visit.

He is playing chess by himself in a coffee shop. I sit down across from him and began to introduce myself.

"Hello, Mr. Dutilleux. My name is—"

"Shh, shh."

"Okay, then."

I sit there awkwardly. A minute later he moves his black king's knight to C3.

Just then, a group of girls walk by. One of them giggles and says in a flirty voice, "Hi Henri," elongating the last "ee" sound as if it will stimulate the dead soul within him. She notices he pays her no mind.

"Well, then!" she huffs, and she runs her hand over the board, spilling the pieces all over the ground. Dutilleux makes a noise not unlike a dying bear. The group of girls burst into laughter then walk away.

"I'm so sorry Mr. Dutilleux, let me help you with that."

"Please, call me Henri. And don't you worry about a thing."

"Wait, did you just quote Stevie Wonder to me?"

He gives a me funny look. "Who?"

The music of Henri Dutilleux is truly phenomenal at every hearing. At once old and new, adventuresome and profound. You really get the sense he is painting a picture, using form to tell a story. Not the typical, self-indulgent "there and back again" nonsense Tolkien stole, something deeper. Something even more primal than Joseph Campbell's *Hero with a Thousand Faces*.

When I ask him about his influences, he tells me, "I listen to the birds."

"Oh, so like Messiaen."

"No, not like Olivier Messiaen. He is wonderfully spectral, but he will listen to birdsong and literally write it down. He is like a cassette recorder using Western music notation. Then he'll plough it all down into a formless, cosmic gumbo, and it is lovely."

"Okay, so what do *you* do with birdsong?"

"I just listen to them. They inspire me to create. Not the sounds themselves, mind you. No, I get inspired by the fact that they make sound at all. I don't try to be like them because I doubt they are trying to be like anyone."

"So, you wouldn't say you are influenced by anyone? Say for instance, a 19th-century German composer?"

"Oh, you mean like Beethoven? I do like him a lot. I think *Opus 101* is one of the greatest piano pieces ever written. I'm sure there is some influence in there. Nothing I can truly trace, though. Why do you ask?"

-six-

Beethoven insists they set up ground rules for the composition to save humanity:

1. The piece will center on a pianistic instrumentation.
2. Each composer will create and elaborate on a narrative for the ideas the *other* composer is to set to music in his own way.
3. The resulting piece will total six movements. Each composer will take credit and ownership of their three respective movements, to return to his own time and call whatever he wills.

My 21st-century readers may be dissatisfied at this point with the details of their composition process. Neither really wants me around, so I spend most of my time playing chess by myself or with one of Beethoven's housemaids. Other times, I peruse Beethoven's extensive library, which is mostly filled with histories.

You can imagine how hard it is for a time traveler to read a history published in the 18th century.

The discussions with the two composers are quite unlike any I've ever experienced. To start off, they both take the revelation of the existence of time travel very well. When I offer Dutilleux a seat in the time machine to travel back one hundred fifty years, he smiles and asks me, "When I come back, will I have aged?"

"No, not at all. Would you believe me to have lived through two hundred earth years?"

"Yet you look to be younger than forty. Very well, that is good to know."

Upon their meeting, both men show little outward excitement with the prospect. They are not rude; they just take this project seriously. No questions from anyone about the other's time or his methods. In fact, after agreeing on the above ground rules, they rarely even talk of music. They are focused on the various small elements within the story they are scoring. It is a volley like one would hear in the writer's room of *Saturday Night Live*.

"Would there be any negative consequence if . . ."

"What do you think spurred Giner to . . ."

"If we agreed to make the villain . . ."

It takes the men three months and five days to finish the work. You may recognize the individual movements as belonging to Beethoven's *Third Piano Concerto* and Dutilleux's *Piano Sonata*, but when played in the originally established order (the third movement of Beethoven's, the third movement of Dutilleux's, Beethoven's first, Dutilleux's second, Dutilleux's first, and Beethoven's second), along with a precisely placed tango-style improvisation and a reference to Leonard Bernstein's "I Have a Love," you will have taken part in the legendary *Planet of the Apes Concerto* for piano and orchestra, my joy to make yarn of Hvensel and Grun's botched attempt.

The work almost completed, we now have to find someone to perform the piece in the 21st century, during the heart of the social equality progression.

We leave Beethoven in the year 1800—he shows no interest in seeing any of the future, saying, "With all due respect, Mr. Poisser, what you do is inhuman and dangerous. I pray for your wellbeing and thank you from my heart of hearts for this honor. I will carry it to the grave as my greatest, most secret accomplishment."

When I drop off Henri Dutilleux, he also shares his contempt of joining me in the search for a worthy performer, though he encourages me to find a young musician. A leader, not an impresario. Dutilleux insists the tango and the *Westside Story* bit have to be done with as much vigor as the rest of the piece—"for it is those sections that will stir within the heart of the listener the will to personally take on the duty of creation."

I was saddened to leave these masters. They represented to me such a foreign way of life, to create out of nothing and to do it so regularly that it becomes not just an expertise, but an identity. It broke my heart to think that I had spent my whole long life without any creative practice. As I shut the door on the machine, for the first time I hummed a melody of my own creation to an audience of no one.

-seven-

Hello.

My name is Rickren y'Stadvenjanesol.

I am the current board president and co-founder of the Society for the Advancement of People with Less Hair.

It is bittersweet, the task I have, to finish this story for you.

Several months ago, the time traveler Henri Poisser returned from a mission we at the SAPLH had sent him on.

His mission was successful. I understand from his recounting as well as bits and pieces of his writings that after leaving Henri

Dutilleux to find a performer for the *Planet of the Apes Concerto*, he spent a very long time in the 21st century until he met a young pianist named Rosario Davez in the year 2015, who took to the project with fervor.

By all accounts, the performance went well. Rosario recruited over thirty of his conservatory friends to play in the orchestra, while he himself conducted from the piano. It was well attended by the Upstate New York community, and Henri Poisser himself stood in attendance on that historic day. The musicians in the audience were greatly moved, critics in their reviews spoke of the inspiring creativity of the young man.

While Henri was concerned that people would not believe the tale of the eccentric time traveler and the eventual rule of the apes, Rosario explained that creativity is not an act of truth, but of faith.

"Even now," said Rosario, "it could be said your tale of the apes is a false one. The future, for me, is unwritten. If what we did here today worked, then it is unwritten for you as well, Mr. Poisser. Besides, can something that has not happened yet really be true or false? If it can be changed, is anything true or false? I hope you will create when you get back to your time, Mr. Poisser."

In the end, the concert young Rosario Davez put on became the first of several impressive concert events throughout his lifetime. His career was an inspiration for many musicians, dancers, and artists alike.

We don't know how Henri Poisser knew this would help the 27th-century musicians in the wake of Giner's death.

Personally, I don't think he knew himself. Like the rest of us, he grew up in a world without new art. When he told us of his conviction about "preparing the vessel," none of us had a clue what he referred to. Yet, if it is true what Rosario Davez said about creativity being an act of faith, then before he even left on his mission, I venture that Henri Poisser was an artist of the purest degree.

When he returned to us, to the year 3038, we instantly knew something was wrong.

The first thing that happens to a time traveler on their return is the implantation of memories. It is an incredible sight to behold. The time traveler gets out of the machine and is immediately surrounded by a purple glow. They open their mouths wide and with each breath, inhale the new memories caused by the effects of whatever their mission was.

Now, I had never before commissioned a time traveler. Fellow board member Wik Raymenkris apparently had seen an implantation happen a few years back, and the rest of us had, of course, seen the process happen only two days before in Hvensel and Grun. Granted, the effects of their mission were nowhere near as impactful as Henri Poisser's.

When Hvensel and Grun went through their implantation, very little happened. They opened their mouths and took in a gulp of air. Once they realized nothing had changed in the society they returned to, they shouted "*fuck*" to high heaven in unison.

When Henri Poisser got out, he immediately received what we all imagine was a lifetime of memories creating art. He fell to his knees and wept inconsolably for almost ten minutes.

Upon his arrival, we did not right away know whether the mission was a success. Since we were only the commissioners, we did not ourselves experience an implantation. It was not until my sister Yulia went to turn on the radio and we heard a song none of us had heard before that we understood what he had done.

It was the most beautiful thing.

While the SAPLH was able to thrive with its renewed vision of expanding arts education for all, the wonderful life and work of Henri Poisser never received the recognition I believe it deserved. Among those of us involved, he will always be a hero of immeasurable worth.

Sadly, one of the unfortunate stereotypes of time travelers is that they eventually go mad, attempting to justify their many implanted memories. Barely a month after his return, he took his own life. His body, overdosed on sleeping pills, was found lying on the floor of his house. The radio was still on, tuned to the classical station. He did not leave a note; he did not share his struggles with any of us.

I am haunted to this day by the notion that Henri Poisser was too old to be sent on such a dangerous mission, yet I cannot help but think that somehow, he knew this would be his last mission, and it brought him only too much joy to see it to fruition.

His sacrifice will not be forgotten.

In memory of Henri Trygstad Poisser
Beloved time traveler, friend, and artist
June 30, 3001–September 15, 3038

HOW TO: THE PIANO BAR

A List of Genius Rules from the World's Fifteenth-Greatest Piano Jockey

1. For Bon Jovi's "Livin' on a Prayer," replace the opening line of the second verse with "Tommy's got a six-inch cock."

2. For the last line of David Bowie's "Space Oddity," sing, "Planet Earth is blue and my testicles are too."

3. If you notice people are not feeling the song you are currently playing, allow yourself to finish at the end of the first chorus in a big, showoff-y fashion so you can at least reward them with a rousing performance of *forte* glissandos. If you know the energy is there but it's currently dormant, do the opposite. Summon forth your most ADHD-adjacent self to play a verse and a chorus of ten songs back-to-back. This will not only beckon the crazy energies that feed your tip bowl, but it will also encourage excitement. "What will he play next?" "*Oh my god, I love this one!*"

4. When you ask people for a request and their answer is, "What is *your* favorite thing to play?" respond with, "Are you sure you

want to hear that? Are you *really sure?*" Just really milk it, and then go to town on The Monkees' "I'm a Believer." If you've already played that song, tell the story of Jason Robert Brown's *The Last Five Years* and play "Shiksa Goddess."

5. If you burp while singing, blame it on Shaquille O'Neal's fried chicken upstairs. It's so good. In reality, singing itself creates air inside your stomach, so it is normal. Also, if you inhale while eating or drinking, you're again creating air inside your stomach. Don't freak out and think something is wrong with you. Don't eat anything for four hours before you sing.

6. Don't play full solo instrumental sections of songs, even if you are as talented as Rosario Davez. The only exception to this is if you are going to do the solo from Styx's "Come Sail Away." Make sure, after that initial A-flat chord, you say something like, "Okay, so I'm just going to goof around here for a little bit. Feel free to talk amongst yourselves." When you're finished and you get back to the C-major section, make sure you are standing up and rocking out like a frikkin' ACDC concert so people start cheering.

7. Every time the waiter or waitress walks into the room, have everyone give them a round of applause. Also make sure you know their names so you don't seem like an ass wipe.

8. If someone requests a song you don't know entirely, play what you do know of it. Find a way to go into another song in a similar key or beat pattern. Then, as a tongue of good faith, reprise the requested song.

9. For Van Morrison's "Brown Eyed Girl," you'll get a cheer for singing, "making love to your big, fat ass" in the third verse.

Also feel free to say "brown-eyed bitch" a few times. But only at the end.

10. Don't be afraid to play a slow song or even a song you know people won't know. This is how you can create a moment. Tell a short story about the slow song and dedicate it to starving children in Michigan or something.

11. You know that stupid trick musicians do with Billy Joel's "Piano Man" where you repeat the line about the bread in the jar until someone gives them money? *Do it every time.* Even if you're playing to a group of kindergartners or poor college kids. You repeat that sucker for thirty minutes if you have to. Don't let them win.

12. Queen's "Bohemian Rhapsody," Gloria Gaynor's "I Will Survive," Journey's "Don't Stop Believing," and Smash Mouth's "All Star" are great songs if you need a vocal break. The audience will sing everything, no worries. Just smile and mouth the words.

13. Offering to do karaoke is also a great way to not have to sing. This will get people in the door as well, but make sure you don't let your show become a karaoke party. After someone sings Adele's "Someone Like You," throw on your cool "Rolling in the Deep"/"Crazy" medley to remind people that *you* are the maharajah.

14. Are you a classical music nerd? Play eight measures from your favorite pieces as a string in a narrative. For instance: someone tells you they love you (Tchaikovsky's *Romeo and Juliet*) but then you have to kill her husband (*Godfather* theme) which makes your lover mad so she leaves you (Beethoven's

"Moonlight Sonata") and then you get with her hot friend Mandy (Kool and the Gang's "Celebration").

15. Theme nights are great. Eighties night is always a jam. Billy and Elton nights are also jam. Broadway nights will make you rich.

16. Don't give boring people attention. Always know what you're going to play next. If you ask someone for a request and they look at you blindly, you can just go into the song you were going to do and ask someone else after that. Allowing an audience member's inability to decide will destroy any momentum you are building.

17. If some idiot requests a song that sucks or doesn't match the energy you want to maintain, say, "Oh yeah, sure, we can do that. But *first* . . ." and play your already-planned next song. Afterward, you can consider their request. This is generally the way you want to go with requests, instead of playing everything right away. This keeps you in control. If it is a god-awful request, just assume everyone forgot it and go on with something better.

18. Even though audiences hate silence and instrumental solos, they *love* suspense. You can build this, for instance, by playing the two lefthand G octaves that open Soft Cell's "Tainted Love" over and over. Do it for longer than seems acceptable, and then once you start the full lick, your audience will come *hard*.

19. You don't usually need to play second verses. No one knows them, and most songs are famous for the chorus anyway. Verse-chorus-bridge-chorus is usually a perfect roadmap and

all you need for people to appreciate a song before they get bored of it. You know how ADHD people get when they are flipping through the radio? Multiply that by eight, and you have the typical piano bar audience. Second verses are harmonically and melodically just a repeat of the first verse, so they will remind people they are bored. Don't remind them.

20. It's not about the tips; it's about the experience. My best-tipped night was over seven hundred dollars, but there were maybe three or four groups in the audience, and only one of them was throwing hundred-dollar bills into the bowl. My best experience was a standing-room-only crowd where people were lining up to do karaoke with me. I made fifty bucks that night. If you only play for tips, most of your career will be a letdown. No one, not even the most intuitive god-man, can know exactly the right song for each crowd, and sometimes the crowd just doesn't have a lot of money to spare. The best you can do is be your authentic self, one hundred percent of the time.

21. Your body and your voice are your moneymakers. If you do not invest in continuous training to strengthen both, your career will have an expiration date. No one can tell you when that will be, but it is certain it'll be at the most inconvenient time.

22. Keep your integrity and uphold a contagious and positive energy.

23. Love your people, and they will love you.

24. No one night will make or break a career.

25. Dream big, stay motivated.

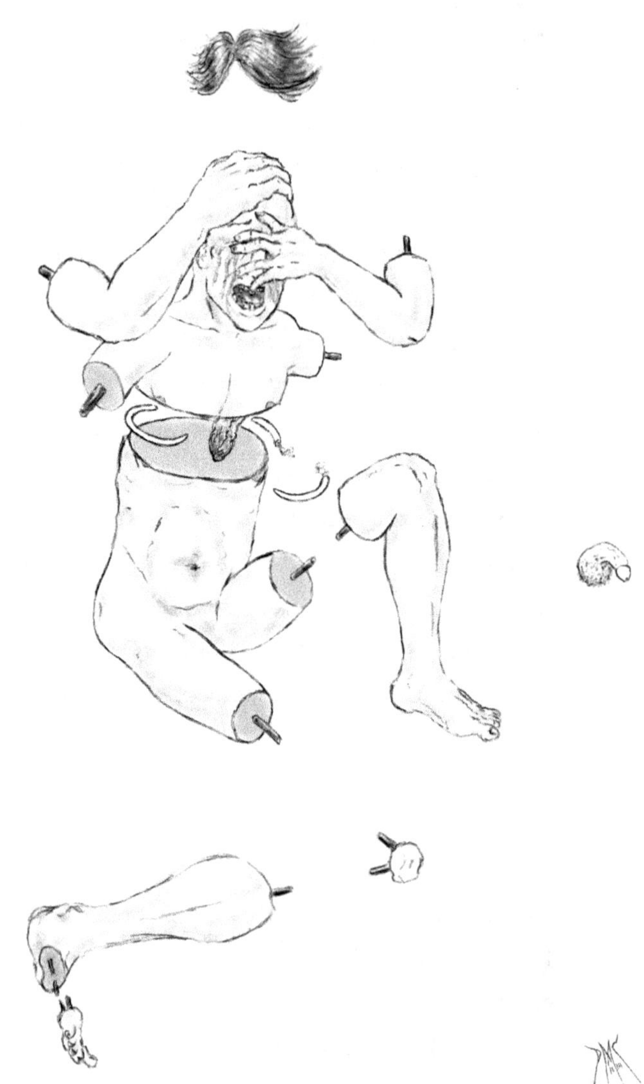

DECONSTRUCTING
THE LOSER

Hi, God.

It's me again.

I don't understand why I am the way I am.

I ran away from music for years because I didn't want to become

a mediocre old man playing kids' shows and community theater

productions, even though I enjoyed doing it immensely.

In those years, I feigned the image of a wealthy businessman,

but in reality, everything I attempted turned to dust.

Is there nothing I can do right?

Now, working in music again, I face the same issues.

Never musical issues—but there is always

something getting in the way.

I call my sound guy a horse cock . . .

I am unsure of a manager's gender and
say so. I lose the contract . . .
When, against all odds, I land a *new* contract to
play music and make great money, I turn around
and offend a diamond-level patron . . .

This morning, I slept through a training—for the second time.
Will they withhold my pay now?
Why do these menial things haunt me? I feel like Moses
at Meribah, whacking a rock instead of speaking to it.
He did everything right, but because of *one* mistake,
You forbade him entry into the Promised Land.
Am I not saved by grace?
Did You forget me?

My wife left me after seven months.
Seven months!
Is there no one who will give me a chance? Am I so despised
among men and women that they look for a way to be rid
of me as soon as I fall short of their standards *one time*?
How is this fair? How can there be people out
there taking advantage of systems and women
who have no talent or heart for the world?
How are *they* driving Cadillacs down San Fernando Square?
How did my world get like this?
In childhood, nothing was impossible. When I was a
"wealthy businessman," nothing was impossible. Now that
I'm back to being a musician, *everything* is impossible.

I am trying to be true to where I am and who I am, but failure
follows me wherever I go and laughs at all my attempts to
fit in within any culture: professional, social, relational.
I hate this, and I'm honestly starting to hate You, God.
Why have You made me this way?
Do You get joy from watching me stumble through
life like a blind pig? An uncontrollable, uncontrolled
flab of flab trying to feel good all the time, succeeding
most of the time but forever plagued by addictions and
depressions, too prideful to be diagnosed and seek help?
I'm tired of all this, God.
Either kill me or start making some sense.
Why would You make me a great musician but limit my
career by the stupidest, most menial shortcomings?
Is that Your idea of a joke?
Make some people brilliant in one way but barely
functional in others? You trying to get me to learn
some hippie interdependence nonsense?
What is the point of that?
All people do is hurt each other. Their smiles are always
fake, not out of malediction but out of confusion,
trying to balance concern for their own well-being
with the desire to not be a selfish dick all the time.
You really think relying on others is going to help me,
God? When they fail me, I'm still the only one who
suffers. Blaming them for my problems won't do any good,
because "I should have known they couldn't be trusted."
Yeah.

Wouldn't it be great if You had given me the
ability to intuit another person's mind?
You can't do that, though, can You, God?
I can hardly understand my own mind at this point.
Guess I'll either trust everyone blindly
and hate them when they fail . . .
or do it all myself and hate myself when I fail.
You have made an awful world, God.
This world sucks.
This life sucks.
I wish it would all go away.
All of it.
Start over.
Count me out.
I'll be more than happy to spend the rest of eternity in non-
existence. Let everyone forget the name "Rosario Davez."

Rosario Davez.
What a loser that guy is.
Let it be gone, let me be gone, let the pain be gone.
Wouldn't have to deal with Your third-
grade attempt at a universe.
In the end, all of this is meaningless. No one
gets out alive, no one gets out unscarred.
Who really needs this agony? Who wins?
Nonsensical, cruel, unfair, rare moments
of light humor. Mostly pain.
Take me away from it all.

Say goodbye to the small joys for me.
The fun moments You allow me.
The undeniable sparkles from the family
and the friends I do receive.
The wonderful smiles from a singer of sweet melody.
The delicious Herbalife milkshakes at the corner shop.
Waking up to the sound of my neighbor's toilet stuck in a
perpetual flush cycle, sounding like two triceratopses having sex.
The subtle victories of all the men I know, trying
to be better for their wives and children.
In tears, I think of the gift of music and the love it creates
in a room. The thousands of people who watch me and take
something special away each night. The moments they cherish.
Sure, I might not be the best artist, but I
create memories. Now *that's* an art.

All the people who call themselves my friend.
Oh, God.
How could I turn my back on them?
Are they not a gift worth living for?
I cannot thank you enough for these people, God.
I love them.
I love You so much, God.
Thank You for listening.
—RD

THE AUCTIONEER'S
DAUGHTER

Late Impressionist. Shades of dark blue in the background contrasting masterfully with the light-blue raindrops of the foreground. A brilliant silver British pavement atop the Edwardian brick road. A single streetlamp, barely holding its own against the darkness around it. The subjects of the work: two young girls, both caught in the rain, both soaked to the bone. One left of center, laughing cheerfully. One jumping in a puddle, arms outstretched.

It is the only work not sold that mid-May afternoon at the estate sale. To celebrate their new acquisitions, the adults make their way outside to the picnic overlooking the massive grounds behind the Corey Mansion.

Sentiments are high surrounding the auction. The Coreys have been a prominent family in the Portland area for generations, yet only six years after the passing of his parents, Matthew Corey, the last surviving heir of the Corey estate, has recently been reported dead in a mysterious happening overseas. While the son does not have much of a reputation among the community, and while the auctiongoers wear sad faces to see the place emptied out, many valuables are sold at remarkable discounts.

As the servants clear the space, the teenage Harriet and Rosario run through the Oregon mansion, trying their hardest to get hopelessly lost.

They are amazed at the number of rooms: thirty-one total. There are ten bedrooms, eight bathrooms, a few offices and dining rooms, and two kitchens. It is in one of these kitchens the two teenagers first kiss. It is a very nice kiss, which gives Rosario the idea to go into every room and recreate it.

As they traverse from room to room, Harriet tells him of her life. As an auctioneer's daughter, she explains, she would travel with her parents to mansions and ballrooms all over the country. The most expensive piece she ever saw sold was a lost painting by the famous Vincent van Gogh.

When she tells him it went for four hundred million dollars, Rosario freezes. She is still walking when she notices his hand slip away. Harriet turns around and laughs, seeing his shocked face. She grabs his hand and yanks to get him to walk; Rosario falls over on his face. Laughing harder now, she hops down to ride his back, shouting:

"Four hundred million dollars for a dead Rosario!"

Rosario finally breaks into laughter himself, not because of what she said, but because her left knee has kicked up into a ticklish spot under his arm. He flips himself over to face the lovely girl straddling him. They only met half an hour earlier.

"I think that's a little too much money for someone to pay just for me."

Harriet thinks for a second. Then, without leaving her strategically gratifying position on top of the boy, she reaches over and picks up a small side table. She lifts it over her head, revealing her lovely thin stomach.

"Four hundred million dollars for a dead Rosario, plus side table!"

"Yes, I think that's a much better deal."

Rosario squeezes her hips and is horrified to discover the noise Harriet makes when she is tickled. It is like something that would come out of a hyena if the hyena were Irish and also burped and hiccupped at the same time.

Unfortunately, Rosario hates burping with a passion. Fortunately, he is really into redheads. He gets an idea.

"Feel free to kiss me in the next room, but you have to stay away from my face."

She furrows a brow, tilts her head to the left, and looks up. Then she gets it.

A kiss.

Somewhere other than his face.

She blushes and smiles wickedly.

Before returning to the grand chamber where the auction was held, Rosario opens the door to the thirty-first and last room. It was once, they assume, a smoking room for the gentlemen. There are empty bookshelves and tables with ornate designs dating back to the twelfth century. The chairs reserved for lounging and discussing politics have been removed, save one large purple monstrosity. It faces a wide window, out of which they see a great lawn where the rich folk are having their afternoon tea. Rosario and Harriet figure they are currently the only people in the building.

Rosario goes to the wall and walks the curtain across the window, leaving a small crack wide enough to let in some light and for them to know when people start heading back inside.

In a prominent corner stands a massive crocodile on its hind legs, terrifying Harriet into a shriek before Rosario shows her the SOLD tag and explains that it is stuffed.

She looks him deep in the eye and whispers, "I'm gonna stuff *you*."

With that, they fall onto one of the tables in an enraptured embrace. Their lips helplessly interlock; Rosario reaches underneath Harriet's blouse to undo her brassiere; she burps into his face.

"You think that's funny, do you?"

Clothes thrown about in all corners of the thirty-first room. They are fervently making love under the watchful eye of the stuffed crocodile when Harriet says worriedly, "Wait . . ."

She reaches down and picks up Rosario's shirt from off the floor and tosses it to cover the crocodile's head. Now they have privacy.

It is a rather thoughtful gesture; if anyone were there to witness the things they do to each other for the next hour, even a stuffed crocodile would certainly perish from the discomfiture.

It is nearing sunset when the rich folk begin their migration inside to grab their coats and head home. Rosario and Harriet, finished and breathless, are pondering the unsold piece of artwork in the grand chamber. Rosario smiles as Harriet points out the two girls in the painting are almost as drenched as they are.

"Why you figure this one didn't sell?" she asks him. "Not even a bid, apparently." She ponders for a moment. "I would have bought it."

"I suppose it possible this crowd does not appreciate the Post-Impressionist sentiment. I like it as well, though I have to admit there isn't very much drama going on. Yes, I understand it is raining, but we're in Oregon, aren't we? It rains all the time. There is no drama between the characters. You've got both girls smiling and enjoying themselves. Where is the tension? How is an artist going to paint two girls but have no tension between them?"

Harriet becomes suddenly quite cold.

"Not everything needs drama, you know!"

She turns and runs to her father, who has just brought in her coat and umbrella.

"Impeccable timing, Father. Shall we go home?"

Rosario reaches into his pocket and takes out the note Harriet scribbled to him earlier that day before the auction began. It is her name and number with a heart sign.

He gets into the car with his mom and dad. As they drive home, they discuss all the fantastic products of the day. His mother won an antique sewing machine, and his father a sixteenth-century rifle from the Middle East.

"What did you guys think of the painting of the two girls in the rain?" Rosario asks.

His mother replies, "Oh, that thing? Gosh. Poor auctioneer stood there awkwardly dropping the initial bid amount, but no one was interested. Hardly worth a hundred dollars."

"You don't think it was a good painting? Like, objectively?"

His father loves when Rosario naively talks about art as if there is such a thing as objective good. "Oh of course. But that lost Van Gogh painting they found a few years ago—you remember that, honey? The one that went for four hundred million? The rich bastard didn't pay that much because it was objectively good, he paid that amount because it was *Van Gogh*."

The car is silent. His dad is right, of course, but Rosario isn't going to say it.

After a minute, his dad asks, "Do you know the story of that painting?" looking at Rosario in the rearview mirror.

He shakes his head.

"It was painted by the auctioneer's daughter, actually. It was a gift to the young man who owned the mansion, before he died, of course. They had been lovers for years, apparently. She begged him not to go off to the war, almost like she knew what would happen to him."

"What did happen? Was he was killed in action?"

"Oh, hardly. From what I heard, it was a rainy night when he got separated from his troop. After losing his battle buddies, he ran around for hours, trying to find them instead of staying put so they could find him—which they eventually did. The next day, they found what little remained of his body in the river. They think he was crossing a rope bridge when he found himself falling into crocodile-infested waters. A terrible way to go if you ask me."

"Wow."

They drive the rest of the way home discussing updated rich-folk gossip when Rosario has his best idea yet.

The next day, Harriet's father lets her know that the painting was indeed bought by a young man in Hillsboro. She looks at the receipt and smiles. He bought it for thirty-one dollars.

She is still smiling when Rosario calls her up and invites her to the *Nutcracker* ballet that night.

JACK RUSSELL TERRIER

Dear Veronica,

I cannot put into words how grateful I am. The last week has been completely transformative for me. What you thought was just a favor, a chore required of people who own animals, was exactly what I needed to get to the next level in this game called life.

Let me start by saying this: you have been such a catalyst in my life. I credit you and no one else with the launch of my music career here in Upstate New York. Working with you at Edison General has been life-altering, picking your brain on how business works invaluable. But I think your support of me as an artist will always be the most meaningful gift you could have given me. The way you introduce me as "the greatest pianist alive" to people you don't even know! Who does that? It is just so cool to know someone who has done the work to be a vessel in the way you have. A lot of people think it is all about being at the right place at the right time, but I think it is deeper than that. To spend one's life actively spreading love and selflessly giving of one's time, expertise, and resources is the single most surefire way to achieve everlasting wealth. The kind they moralize in It's A Wonderful Life.

But I digress. Back to your Jack Russell Terrier.

I ask myself: Was it just a Facebook post? A coincidence I logged on at the right time to be the first person to respond? Maybe that thing we call "accident" is God's way of entering into our lives to make sure our next step is the right one.

You see, all my life, I've been terrified of animals. I could admire them from a distance, but I saw little value in their being. Certainly, their existence was not and would not ever be of any significance to my life.

But dogs were another story: there was simply no way we could coexist.

I remember going to friends' houses and being greeted by their dogs. The patter of their energetic feet on the hardwood floor, usually accompanied by ferocious barking, and typically, if they were big enough and not afraid of humans enough, violently shoving their noses right into the front of my pants. To hide my horror, I would make the joke that if I greeted women like that, I'm certain I would have so many more friends than I do now.

The absolute worst of these encounters was when the dogs were skinny and bouncy. These motherfuckers could jump and lick my face. And the owners, my "friends," would say in a calm but sturdy voice, "Lucian, no," or, "Gus Gus, down."

My reaction has always been the same: I would bury my hands in my face. Never gave it much thought. I just assumed

I was afraid of dogs and this was a common response, as some-one who just naturally didn't like dogs. That is, until I was twenty-three years old.

I do not remember the context, but somewhere in con-versation during a family get-together, my mother revealed to everyone.

"Oh, yeah. Rosario used to be a dog person, but ever since a pup bit him in the hand when he was five years old, he's been terrified of them."

I had no idea! I pressed her for details. Apparently, a neighbor had a mutt named Azabache that all us kids on the block would play with. Mom said that I was especially close with the mutt; sometimes while the other kids were playing kickball or something, I would run around with Azabache by myself. We would climb trees together, go into the swamps, play fetch. All that stuff.

This was wild to me because I had no recollection of any of this. Understandable, since I was so small, but still! Five years old is not too young to remember.

And so, at twenty-three years old, I, Rosario Davez, dis-covered I had suppressed memories.

And to be honest, this really messed with me. Not sure what it is, but I suppose I thought to myself, how could I expect to live a life of love when I am unable to accept love from one of God's creatures?

It seemed hypocritical of me to want to show love to everyone but not accept love from dogs. I don't know. Maybe I'm crazy. But that's how I felt.

So, when you shared your post on Facebook about needing someone to dog sit your Jack Russell Terrier, the aptly named "Russell," for a week, well, I jumped on it. Aggressively. Like a Jack Russell Terrier would.

And what a week it was!

I knew it would be hard, but I had also learned from my time working at Edison General the best and sometimes only way to get over a fear is to immerse yourself in it, to prove you can thrive in it.

The first day was rough. Russell barked at me like I was the Antichrist. He was so mad or scared or whatever that even though I had the door open for him to go outside, he just peed right there on the kitchen floor. At that point, he stopped barking. I guess dogs can't bark and pee at the same time. But now I was angry!

Eventually, he stopped barking long enough for me to go into the fridge and get him some burger treats, which shut him up long enough for me to mop the floor.

Frikkin' Russell.

He calmed down after that, but it started up again as soon as I got in bed to sleep. This was the ultimate test for me. That first night, I was not going to have it, so I closed the door. But the other nights, I let him in, and I swear to God, I'll never understand the amount of pleasure this dog gets from licking!

I mean, don't get me wrong. I love a good licking as much as the next guy, but jeez. So violent. Made me feel so embarrassed when I realized that all those times a girl called me a puppy after spending the night, I don't think they were giving me a compliment.

Walking Russell was special. This was an aspect of dog ownership I understood. Having a dog makes talking to girls easy. What I did not expect was for this racist motherfucker to start hollering at every little black girl we passed on the street!

Frikkin' Russell.

Anyway. Just wanted to share that with you, Veronica. Now I can go into anyone's house and get down and dirty with any dog I meet. Still terrified of other animals, but I'm good with one species for now. Not trying to turn myself into Steve Irwin over here.

Rosario

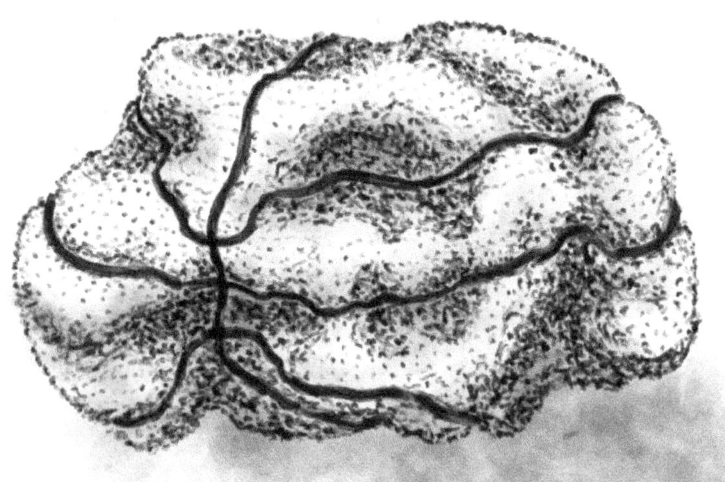

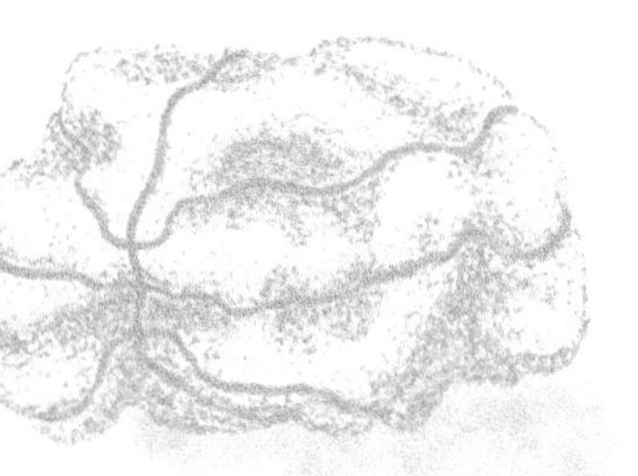

THE DIAMOND OF THE THORN

Histories

The last distribution of the Diamonds occurred in modern-day Palestine nearly two thousand years ago. The cast of hosts was as follows:

Diamond of the Breath: Judas Thaddeus
Diamond of the Step: Simon Peter
Diamond of the Horn: John the Baptizer
Diamond of the Thorn: Jesus of Nazareth, the Christ

You can read their story within the first four books of the Christian New Testament. It is a phenomenon, a glorious and true tale, which we will not revisit here. *Nota bene*: no testaments of either the Christ Himself nor any of his followers detail the following transitional event that set the stage for the next gathering of Diamonds.

After the sacrifice and resurrection of Jesus of Nazareth but before He rose to heaven and took a hard left to start a church in the Americas, He gathered the four Diamonds and prayed earnestly on where to bury them. Jesus knew the world would wait for centuries before another crisis would warrant the need to birth the diamonds anew, so their hiding spots had to be precisely designated to handle the changing of the times.

The Diamond of the Breath, to be born into a passionflower in the Pacific Northwest region of the Americas, had the unique desire to transform herself into a young girl. Thus, Jesus did not bury her at all. For two thousand years, soil would grow over her with the intention of choking her out. But like so many women, all the world threw at her to keep her down became fertile ground for her blossoming.

Of course, years of violence without respite can hardly produce such inspiration as is required of the Diamond of the Breath. So, when young Annika Le Roux picked up the passionflower on a fateful walk with her parents, none of them could have imagined the significance of this introduction. But in those thirty-six hours, the family showed that flower so much love, and as the minutes trickled by toward the end of the *passiflora*'s bloom, the Breath allowed herself to be reborn as the human girl Klara Le Roux.

The Diamond of the Step, always trying to outdo herself, revealed to Jesus her desire to be born in the weirdest possible way. As she explained the plan, Jesus lovingly rolled His eyes so much, He reportedly had a hard time getting back to normal.

"Bury me deep, deep, deep in the sands of the Caribbean. Let the waves pound me into oblivion, that I may be swallowed up by the fish. May the stomach acids dissolve me into further nothingness. I will survive—I am the Diamond of the Step. Let this process take the full two thousand years, so when the time comes, a little boy playing on the beach will take an accidental gulp of sea water and notice not that he has ingested anything other than yucky, yucky whale wash."

Jesus laughed. "Good heavens, Step. Then what, you wish to come out the natural way?"

"You know, humans tend to think of certain orifices as worse than others. I never understood that. No, I will not come out the natural way. Not due to any feelings of disgust I may have, it would just be such a ridiculous farce to, after all this work, have me flushed away with the excrement. No, I'll make my way up to his head and when the time is right, plop myself out the ear."

The Diamond of the Horn, like Breath, also chose to be born as a flower in the Pacific Northwest, but shared with Jesus no secret path to take, or even an intended host.

"Frankly, Jesus, I've found that I have the easy job. Turns out, when you give someone their heart's desire, a lot of other things start falling into place for the rest of the world too. Leave me within communication's reach of Breath; I do get bored between nativities."

The Diamond of the Thorn, meanwhile, had Jesus take her away to a landlocked region of the European continent, in modern day Chernivtsi Oblast, Ukraine.

Anton Hansen

Now it's time for me to tell you about young Anton Hansen, best friend to Rosario Davez, a violinist who had as much energy as the wild Rosario, if not more.

Anton was playing for a crowd at the Upstate New York Lilac Festival when Rosario first saw the young paramount. Feeling it

was time for an introduction, Rosario went down to the front of
the stage and began to dance overenthusiastically to Anton's cover
of Silk Sonic's "Leave the Door Open."

Immediately the two Diamond spirits connected, though
none the wiser to this connection between them. In the middle
of the concert, in front of hundreds of people, Rosario and Anton
began talking about mutual friends, performances they could do
together, and so on.

Within the week, Rosario and Anton played their first concert together. Neither had ever made music so passionately with
another being. After they moved in together a few weeks later,
they discussed how previous musical projects consisted of them
throwing out joules upon joules of energy while their collaborators
sleepily played along. Not anymore.

"You know, bro, I'm serious when I say this. I have never made
music with someone who has as much energy as me, if not more."

"Right back at you, my man! It feels so great."

The two were unstoppable. Hardly any rehearsals were needed
as both were so attuned to each other's musical styles and ideas.
Eventually, they formed a band with some other musicians. With
Anton as the soloist and Rosario the conductor, they were loved
by the community. Venues were packed to the brim to see these
two masters go back and forth. Concert halls all over Upstate New
York that had not made money in years were finally coming to life;
everyone was in love.

A rockstar's paradise, these two lived. Their apartment saw parties every night, their beds saw various women just as frequently.

After one particularly debauched night, the two men are sitting on the couch laughing at their favorite TV show, *Brooklyn 99*:

ROSARIO: You know, I wish I had your vision for my life when I was your age.

ANTON: Hey, man, it's all good. I'm twenty-three, you're twenty-nine. What's a number?

ROSARIO: Yeah, you're right. I just feel like I spent so much time away from music, I think about how much further I'd be right now if I hadn't gotten so afraid of turning out like old Daisy Wilkinson.

ANTON: It is what it is, man. You've had a hell of a journey; don't take that away from yourself.

ROSARIO: And your journey is just getting started, king. How did you get so focused at such a young age?

ANTON: Well, my parents made me practice as a kid, obviously. No kid actually likes to practice, so thank God for parents that don't listen to their children's wishes.

ROSARIO: Amen to that.

ANTON: But I love to play, and it's what I was meant to do. Now, I'm not going to just play with anyone, and I refuse to play somewhere or with someone who does not respect me or my art. Hell, I'd rather play on the streets. Which honestly, is what I was doing until this summer when I suddenly started making all these friends outside of school. I know I definitely have you to thank for that party on the beach where you introduced me to Kevan and all those other people too.

ROSARIO: Whatever, man. You would have been discovered with or without me. Plus, you're the one out there pounding the pavement and getting us gigs, so you've more than paid me back.

ANTON: I know. You're right. Bro, you and me, we're the best in the world at what we do. To answer your question, my life has always been a straight path of music making. My goal is to play for as many people as possible. I never understood why people complicate life. Though, in everyone's defense, I kind of am the host to the Diamond of the Thorn, so I believe I don't really have a choice.

ROSARIO: Um, is that something I am supposed to know about?

ANTON: You mean to tell me that you don't? (*Rosario stares blankly.*) Bro.

ROSARIO: Are you like, a big deal or something?

ANTON: No. I mean, yes. I mean, I guess I just assumed you knew about the Diamonds, since you're such a spiritual guy. Even non-spiritual people *know* about the Diamonds, even if they don't believe in them.

ROSARIO: You wanna go ahead and tell me?

ANTON: Bro! The Diamonds of Old? The heroes of the planet? There's the Diamond of the Breath, the selfless catalyst, carrying the solemn duty to set captives free in body, soul, spirit. You've never heard of this? The Diamond of the Step, traversing all terrains, material and immaterial. The Diamond of the Horn, strengthening the host to fulfil the heart's deepest desire. And me, hosting the Diamond of the Thorn to the gathering and reburying of the diamonds, through my sacrifice.

ROSARIO: Your what?

ANTON: My sacrifice, Rosario! I'm going to die playing the violin to save the world.

ROSARIO: This is too much. What on earth are you talking about?

ANTON: You know the Gospels of Jesus Christ, right?

ROSARIO: Come on, man.

ANTON: Judas Thaddeus was the Breath. Simon Peter was the Step, John the Baptist was the Horn . . .

ROSARIO: And what, Jesus was the—what did you call it, the Thorn?

ANTON: Well?

ROSARIO: I mean, this sounds like just a unique analysis of various characters of the Bible and their roles. Are you calling yourself Jesus?

ANTON: No, no, no. Jesus is God and He came to earth to die for our sins because humanity was lost. But part of Jesus taking on human form was having Him participate in the things of the world. The Diamonds aren't something higher than God. He created them and gave them purpose and distributes them as He pleases. So, when Jesus came down, wouldn't it make sense to align it with a gathering of the Diamonds?

ROSARIO: If you are asking me to interpret a brand-new piece of worldview and theology that I am still convinced is just a weird, jewel-lover mythology . . .

At this point, Rosario thinks back to that piano lesson with Christa Nylssen, where he had a headache and she pulled out a diamond from his ear. He stands up and walks over to his desk, where he has kept it. He's never really thought much of it over the years. But as it has been so long since he has seen Christa, he always brings it with him whenever he has moved, as a memento of his favorite teacher.

Rosario opens the drawer and takes it out. It is dusty but undeniably beautiful. As he holds it, he feels renewed energy and wants to go for a walk. He turns to Anton, eyes huge and face looking the way a Coca Cola bottle feels after it's been vigorously shaken.

ANTON: Oh. My. JESUS-LOVING-GOD-FEAR-ING-GOAT-SUCKING-MOTHER-DOBRE-

HALF-OF-AN-AVOCADO-PIECE-OF-LIME-DISEASE-CARRYING-JIZZ-TREE-CLIMBING-SALAMANDER-MUCUS-GRANDMOTHER'S-GRAVE.

They burst out laughing. Tears of joy and shouts of ecstasy. The meeting of two Diamonds is always a joyful occasion, but in all the millennia of humans walking the earth, there has never been a more jubilant reunion.

Far across the country, in the great state of Oregon, Klara Le Roux looked up and smiled. The time had come.

Lessons

The discovery that he is the host to the Diamond of the Step comes initially as a shock to him, though for some reason it is the new happiest moment of Rosario's life. It soon turns to grief and anger, however, as he realizes Christa Nylssen and his father must have known about this but never once told him anything.

"There's no time for you to be angry, bro," says Anton. "We have to get you up to speed on what this means."

(If you ever see your friend getting angry, maybe don't tell him there's no time to be angry.)

Instead of exploding, Rosario takes a breath and responds, "Okay. Wait, wait. So how old were you when you discovered that you were a host?"

"Well, I didn't mean to. One day when I was seven years old, I went outside with my brother, Marcus. We had already started violin lessons, but my parents were not very strict with us yet, so they would let us play. It was very windy that day, and we were playing basketball. At one point during our game, Marcus threw the ball way too high. It bounced off the hoop, then the wind pushed it hard against a wall, and it ricocheted onto the top of our neighbor's car.

"The ball dented the roof pretty bad, triggering the alarm to go off. We ran over to the ball, which was still bouncing around as if it has a mind of its own. Then our neighbor, Vladimir Kovalenko, came out. He was always a grumpy man, but when he came out and saw what we had done to his car, he let out a roar like a black bear. He took out his knife; my brother and I went running back home. We though he was going to try to kill us. Then we heard him laughing maniacally as he stabbed the basketball and the air let out in one short *whoosh*.

"'And stay away!' he said.

"I got so mad. I ran back to retrieve my ball, angry tears in my eyes. Kovalenko slammed the door behind him before I could get to him. Sniffling, I picked up the remains of the ball. As I carried it back home, I found that inside there was this black, diamond-looking thing. I reached inside to take it out and get a closer look, and as soon as I did, I felt this sudden urge to go play the violin.

"Marcus had already gone up to our parents to tell them what happened. They were about to go to Kovalenko's house when they saw me come inside with the ball. I put it down, picked up the violin, and started playing. Not that I had any clue, but my parents looked at me as if I was glowing. They sat down and listened as I played "Czardas," then gave me a standing ovation when I finished."

"'My God, Anton,' said my dad. 'How did you get so good all of a sudden?' My dad turned to my mom. 'You'd think he was the host to a Diamond of Old, playing like that!'

"Actually, Rosario, thinking about how I'm introducing you to Diamondlore reminds me of how I was introduced myself. I asked my father what he meant by 'Diamond of Old,' and as he was explaining it, I reached into my pocket and pulled out the Diamond I had just found in the deflated basketball! My parents shrieked with excitement!

"That day, quite forgetting what had happened with old Vladimir Kovalenko, they sat me down and taught me everything, just as I'm about to do for you."

With that, Anton proceeds to tell Rosario about the Diamonds. It is an intense evening, but they cover the various attributes of the Diamonds and what they can accomplish within their hosts. Since such a long time has passed since the previous Diamond distribution, not much has been written recently about Diamondlore

Basically, what people call "diamonds" are really ancient, immortal creatures. They exist in the most extreme environments for millions of years in an ever-hardening, ever beautifying process. Sometimes, humans will extract these diamonds from the earth and cut them into shapes in order to make themselves achieve a look of high status. Since humans exist for such a short time, how-ever, the diamonds themselves don't really mind this, and often appreciate the break from sitting in the dirt to sit atop a wealthy woman's bosom.

Eventually though, the humans die or the jewelry is lost to the elements, and at that point, the diamonds can go back to their continual hardening and beautifying. Ideally, all diamonds strive for the point where they possess magical properties.

Now, dear reader, understand that what you call "magic" is usually just something you cannot currently explain, be it a card trick, sleight-of-hand, or illusion. The true magic that diamonds seek, however, are elements of humanity in the abstract. Elements such as bravery, love, freedom, sacrifice. These things cannot be explained from any perspective; that is the real magic!

The Reverend Martin Luther King's sense for freedom, the sacrifice paid by all those soldiers in countries all over the world, the way a stranger stands up to a man bullying another: magic is happening all over the planet. It is inherently unexplainable, and in its manifestation it can surprise the most omniscient beings in existence. Think on how two souls as unassuming as Frodo Baggins and Samwise Gamgee are gifted the courage to travel through dangerous lands, suffering starvation and exhaustion. Who can explain it? Where does magic come from?

ANTON: The Diamonds of Old: the Breath, Step, Horn, and Thorn. Of all the diamonds in existence, these four have attained that sacred magic and as such are called in times of crisis to gather together diffident bands of humans to bring order back to the progression of things.

ROSARIO: Wow, Anton. What am I supposed to do with this information?

ANTON: You know, I asked my parents the exact same thing.

ROSARIO: And?

ANTON: Just live your life, bro. The time will come when I die playing the violin. You are the Step. If I were you, I would do everything. You've already nailed basically every type of music, and you have a few years of financial advisory and real estate success. What else have you always wanted to do, but were afraid to? How can your life be different now that you know you cannot fail?

ROSARIO AND ANTON
SAVE THE WORLD

It's a week later that Rosario gets a phone call from Klara Le Roux, his high school sweetheart.

He sees her name on the phone and answers.

"Wow."

"I know."

"Unexpected—good timing, though."

"Rosario, I have something important to tell you."

"This seems to be the week for it."

"I am the Diamond of the Breath."

There was a commercial a while ago on TV. It showed a man going to a club and purchasing a Bud Light, which triggered the attention of about five hot women. The next scene showed him with these girls on his lap pouring the beer all over themselves in slow motion. They went to leave the club and were greeted by a couple of bouncers who were guarding some famous Johnny

Depp-type guy, who invited them all into his private jet, where there were more Bud Lights and hot women. The jet dropped them off outside this massive sex garden, and they took a limo up to a billion-dollar mansion in the Hamptons. All the while, Eddie Money's "Two Tickets to Paradise" was playing. All because the guy bought a Bud Light.

Rosario feels like this man.

"Klara, this is insane. I just found out I am host to one of the Diamonds, and my best friend Anton hosts the Thorn."

"Exactly why I am calling."

"So, are we all—*cómo se dice*—'psychically linked' now? How did you know?"

"Rosario, it's been a long time since we chatted and there's a lot I have to tell you. Is it okay if I just tell you the story and then you can ask questions after?"

"Wow, Klara, I don't remember you being this forward." He can hear her smile over the phone. "Go ahead."

"Okay. So first, I need you to understand I am not a host like you. I actually *am* the Diamond of the Breath."

Rosario makes one of those confused Jim Halpert faces toward a non-existent film crew.

"Nothing? Okay, I guess I don't have to explain."

"Actually, some backstory on that little detail would be greatly appreciated."

"There it is. Okay, so two thousand years ago, I was picked up by Judas Thaddeus, one of the twelve disciples of Jesus the Christ. You've heard of him?"

"Thaddeus or Jesus? Yes, go on."

"Then you probably already know Jesus himself hosted the Thorn, John the Baptizer hosted the Horn, and Simon Peter had the Step. That was by far the most special, most sacred gathering of our existence, as we were blessed to be intimately involved with our Heavenly Father's plan for the redemption of mankind."

"Klara, are you millions of years old?"

"Yes. Shut up. As you know, the story goes that John the Baptizer was born about three months before his cousin, Jesus. He discovered his Diamond right before his twenty-fifth birthday, which gave the Horn a few years to do her job of granting him his heart's desire.

"You see, John had always wanted to be a priest, like his father Zechariah. The Horn showed him that was not his heart's desire, however. All the priests from the time of Aaron the Levite to then? All of their duties and rituals and sacrifices were designed to point to the long-awaited Messiah. But John, ever since he'd been a baby, even from the womb, knew that Jesus was the Christ, come from God to save the world. He was the one. So, what would the point of another priest be?

"With this realization, John became the Baptizer and started a brand-new ministry of repentance, centered around the idea that the Messiah was coming and was now here, and the people were to ready themselves for the new kingdom He was to bring. This was his heart's desire."

Rosario is eating all this up.

"Okay, so basically, the Horn gave John his heart's desire, which was to be the messenger who would prepare the way for the Lord." He can hear Klara nodding over the phone.

"Exactly," she says. "Now, around that time, I allowed myself to be discovered by Judas Thaddeus, a sweet man whom I believe embodied the spirit of setting the captives free."

"Pause. Real quick, can you explain what 'setting the captives free' means? Anton used those words as well, but I still don't get it."

"Well, much like the confusion among the Jews that the Messiah would be someone warrior-like, many humans think that setting the captives free is about getting rid of earthly tyrants and oppressive regimes. Of course, this is an important and worthwhile cause. But no man is free who is a slave to himself, and I have always dedicated myself to setting people free to do their Genesis mandate: to *create*.

"As God created Adam and Eve, so are humans destined to create, and the Genesis mandate to go forth and multiply does not simply refer to the creation of other humans. Art, too, has a life of its own. As much as the world needs people, it needs art as the grandchild of creation to take on a life of its own, so that humanity can learn the wonderful relationship between maker and the sentience made. Does that make sense?"

"Yeah, actually. That's really cool."

"I think so, too. So together, Thaddeus and I went around loving people and sparking that creativity in everyone. People like Matthew the tax collector. He was kind of like you, Rosario. Scared away from his true passion of writing. But, like you, his was a story of redemption into art. The fact that his gospel opens up the New Testament is a tribute to the power of being set free."

"Now, Simon Peter hosted the Step, just like you. He started out as a fisherman, then quickly made his way into Jesus's inner circle. After Christ's death, he took seriously his calling as 'Rock on which the church is built.' Everything he set his audacious mind to, he achieved."

Even though some of this is a review of things Anton shared with Rosario, he appreciates hearing it again from his old love. One thing still troubles him, though.

"Cool, cool. Now Klara, I'm still confused about the fact that you yourself are a Diamond."

She sighs with all the patience of an ancient being. "There's really not much to it, Rosario. Your Diamond is a living creature too. If she wanted to, the Step could be a human, a cow, an ostrich. I always wanted to try my hand at humanity, and decided I would use this 21st-century distribution to experience it."

"But how can you be a Diamond? You have a daughter."

"Sylvia is full human, just like Arnoux."

"Ugh. That guy."

"You're still bothered by that, huh?"

"No. Though, you being a Diamond is making me wonder how you can justify your choice of any husband, let alone someone like Arnoux Webber."

"Seems like you really want an explanation."

An awkward silence.

"You're not wrong, Rosario. I was more than content with spending my human life away from any romantic ironies. In fact, if you had asked me twenty years ago, I would have explained how it would be impossible for a Diamond to love a human. I would have cited Pygmalion: my influence on people is inevitable, any man I pursue or allow to pursue me will inevitably be changed, thus nixing any element of true love. How could I claim to romantically love someone, knowing that I was the one to create them, in a way?"

Another awkward silence.

"Do you know why you hate Arnoux, Rosario? It's because he has what you've always wished you had, and what allowed me to fall in love with him. Arnoux creates without impulse, without spur. Of the billions of men alive at any given moment, only a handful are so intrinsically stimulated. Not by money or fame or insecurity, but by *love* is my Arnoux motivated. I knew, regardless of my influence, that this man would create, and it would be beautiful. This is deep down why you hate him. You envy his ability to be genuine in his art, though you are cut from the same cloth!"

Rosario shrinks in embarrassment.

"It's okay. Now I know why you were scared away from music, Rosario. It wasn't because you were scared of becoming like an old PTA mom. You got scared away from music because you *wanted* to be. You *wanted* an excuse to be average. And if you didn't pursue music, you'd never be great, because you were afraid of being great. But you *are* great, and nothing you do will keep that from being true. That is why the Step chose you to be her host. That is why I am calling you today."

They say nothing for a while. Klara can hear muffled sobs on the other line, but she does not want to interfere. Rosario rarely feels so understood as when he speaks with Klara, and it breaks his heart how he has allowed such a great distance to come between them.

"I don't know what to say, Klara. You are right, of course. It moves me deeply to hear you talk like this. I have so much regret."

"I wish you wouldn't, my friend."

They sit in silence again.

After about a minute, Anton returns to the apartment with a loud slam of the door and, as usual, a loud "*My man!*"

Snapping out of it, Rosario uses this opportunity to introduce the two, and the three of them stay up late, chatting into the evening about life and beauty, about the various ways the Diamonds have influenced things. Anton plays his violin for her, ecstatic to the bone about meeting another Diamond. They all wonder if there will be an opportunity for the four to get together anytime soon.

"I know the Horn was taken a few years after my sister Annika picked me up in my *passiflora* state," says Klara. "We were both born in neighboring fields in Oregon, but whoever is hosting the Horn took her far away, I don't know where."

"So, you're not psychically linked?" Rosario asks.

"No, no. But the Horn is like that. Exists rather independently from the rest of us, believing that the granting of one heart's desire unlocks the chain of all redemptive events. A bit cheeky if you ask me. But I could not prove her wrong. Where would the world be if the Horn had not moved John the Baptizer to go off into the desert so he could later baptize the Christ? That the Christ in turn could go into the desert and defeat the Devil's temptations?"

"I hope to meet her one day," says Anton. "Though maybe we already have, huh?"

"Maybe."

Rosario and Anton live together in Upstate New York for half a year longer before Anton's student visa expires and he is forced to go back home to Chernivtsi Oblast, Ukraine.

All that time after the discovery of the Diamonds is spent much like before, making music and partying. They keep in touch with Klara—Rosario certainly does not want to lose that friendship again. He grows to respect Arnoux Webber as an artist and person. He even becomes grateful that Klara is able to have a fulfilling life with the man.

It is thanks to Anton that Rosario can have a successful music career after his five-year stint as an energy-rebate-specialist-slash-financial-advisor-real estate-mogul. Anton introduces him to an agency that supplies musicians for theme parks. Rosario will be fired after only two weeks on the job, but this will prove to be for the best, as his real talent lies in playing on cruise ship piano bars.

His first gig aboard the *CSS Radhames* is to begin toward the end of January of 2022, right around the same time Anton is to leave the United States. Upstate New York is sad to lose these two young men, and the parties only intensify as the date of their departure nears. Anton and Rosario are sad as well, though they know their lives and careers will only skyrocket as they move forward.

And skyrocket they do, for lack of a better word.

Within two weeks of Anton's return to his home country, the neighboring President of Russia declares war on Ukraine and begins bombing the people unprovoked. Almost overnight, the peace-loving Slavs of Kyiv are turned into refugees, seeking asylum from the power-mad Vladimir Putin.

While the President of the United States, along with the leaders of the North Atlantic Treaty Organization, flounder about on how to deal with this senseless violence, the friends and fans Anton developed during his short time in New York rally together to bring aid to the Ukrainian refugees. Through various streamed performances, Anton raises over twenty thousand dollars.

Rosario's connections to black-market smuggling routes attempt to find an escape for Anton, to circumvent regulations mandating all men between the ages of eighteen and sixty to remain within the boundaries of Ukraine until the war is over. Though the offer is tempting, Anton is determined not to sully his good standing with any nation-state, as he needs to return to the United States in less than a year to continue his studies. Instead, Anton figures he will make the best out of the situation and do what he does best: play the violin.

He and his brother Marcus play out in the streets for the people of Kyiv for as long as it is feasible. Eventually, the bombing gets so bad in the city that the brothers move back to their hometown, Chernivtsi Oblast. Regardless of where they go, however, the brothers are a hit. People come out in droves to hear them play, their souls forgetting and transcending the horrors going on around them.

Over time, other musicians join the brothers in their outdoor performances. In an interview a couple of years after the war, a young Ukrainian composer named Kirvynal Giner will recount:

"Before the war, it seemed many musicians, including myself, had given up hope that we would ever play again. As unprecedented as the Russian president's attacks were, it really didn't change the fact that things were not going well in the world of art anyway. While the rest of the world scoffed at the way Americans pumped their food up with additives and

preservatives, no one batted an eye at the heartless music we were pumping into ourselves. Everyone seemed to be just looking for the next sick beat to twerk and get drunk to; it felt like no one was making genuine art anymore. I know now that this wasn't the case, but—forgive the eccentric comparison— when all you eat is chicken nuggets, you think to yourself, Why would I ever go back to bone-in-chicken?

"Anton and Marcus, louder than anyone else, I think, demanded appreciation. Not insecurely, mind you. But every day and without fail, they would go out into the streets and play. The first few days, hardly anyone was outside for fear of the bombs. Eventually, though, the people started to come outside. I tell, you there was no fear in those men. But what else could be expected? There was no fear in their music!

"More than anything, it is this fact that keeps alive the memory and legacy of Anton Hansen. Wars come and go; there is always someone alive when the dust settles. When Anton made music, it was the real, raw, genuine him. It was not a desire to please his parents, it was not this mechanical performance that would have won him a job in an orchestra. There was no concept of 'right and wrong technique or interpretation' to discuss with a college music professor. This was true of him during the war, it was true of him before the war, whether playing music in America alone with a Bluetooth speaker or with the pianist Rosario Davez.

"I believe we are entering a new era of creation, and I can think of no better tribute to Anton and Marcus than to continue in my own art with bold authenticity."

It is six months after the March 8, 2022 bombing of Chernivtsi Oblast. Rosario is sitting in the apartment he and Anton shared for those few months. He gets a phone call. Looking down, it is Klara Le Roux, his high school sweetheart. He puts the phone up to his ear and doesn't say anything.

A few seconds pass.

"Let's go to Puerto Rico," she says.

Rosario is a broken man like he never thought possible. The toothpaste ran out a month ago, so he has been using a wet toothbrush and nothing else. The soap also ran out; he's been using shampoo on his body the days he feels worthy enough for a shower. A year ago, he bought an ungodly amount of paper towels, which now double as his toilet paper, but he's on the last roll. Rosario and Klara haven't talked since the news came of Anton's death.

This sudden invite feels like someone throwing the curtains open and flooding a dark room with the eleven a.m. sun. After a few attempts, his dry mouth spills out a word.

"Sure."

Rosario is once again impressed with Klara's forwardness. She refuses to explain anything, which is appreciated, as Rosario's depression makes it so he doesn't want to ask a lot of questions. The most he can bring himself to do is pack his luggage, and even that he puts off until an hour before he has to get to the airport.

When he gets off the plane at the San Juan Airport, Rosario goes to the baggage claim where he sees Klara waiting for him, but she is not alone. Next to her stands a mature, tall, and lovely woman in a yellow tracksuit, her lush brown hair up in traditional Ukrainian fashion.

After the two longest hugs he has given anyone in years, Rosario Davez, Klara Le Roux, and the great witch Christa Nylssen make their way out of the airport to a restaurant for lunch.

Three humans sit around the table.

One plump and depressed. One young and lovely. One old and lovely.

Three Diamonds lie on the table.

One black and sparkling. One black and dirty. One black and gold.

"Remember the day we discovered the Step in your ear? In our piano lesson?"

Rosario nods. A moment passes.

"After you left, I went to check on mine. She had gone from pure black to having this single gold line across it. Like a level up, a streamer for achieving a goal. You can see Anton's diamond has a similar thing. When you lived with him, his Diamond didn't sparkle like this, did it?"

Rosario doesn't respond. Another moment passes. Klara puts her hand on his. He brushes it away.

"Ros—"

"Why are we here?"

His sudden alertness startles the two women.

"I get all of this. Anton said it would happen; he would die and his sacrifice would save the world or some bullnads. So what? Doesn't seem like the world is saved to me—or am I missing something?"

"*Papito.*"

The word is spoken in the closest thing to magic either Klara or Rosario have ever heard. In an instant, Rosario is an eight-year-old boy again. All the crying he did alone in his apartment has left only a single tear in his body. It falls at this moment, and Rosario leans in to let Christa Nylssen hold him. After all these years, she still wears the same perfume. She knows perfectly well how to handle the person of Rosario Davez.

"I know you know, *mi vida*. We're not here to insult your intelligence."

"But I *don't* know what to do, *Madrina*! I feel paralyzed. How can I create or do anything in this world that so easily kills its artists?"

"This has always been an art-killing world, Ros . . ."

Klara has put her arm over the embrace of the godmother and godson . . .

". . . and it always will be."

"So, what's the point?"

At this point, Christa Nylssen gently removes herself from the embrace. Klara takes the cue.

"That *is* the point. That you continue to create art, knowing that the world will kill it." There is almost a smile on Klara's face as she says this. "There can be no war without enemies, no hero without villains. Go out and fight."

Christa grabs Rosario's Diamond. "Feel how hot it is." She places it in his hand. He is shocked, but not by the heat. The Diamond of the Step is shaking, not unlike a cell phone overheating. He drops it back onto the table.

"Is it about to explode?"

The women giggle.

"You could say that."

Rosario adjusts himself in his seat, losing his slouch and attempting to match the energy of his Diamond sisters. He looks at them with love. Though the grief from Anton's death will follow him as long as he lives, Rosario feels grateful for the accountability the women are gently but firmly holding him to. He swallows and forces out a determined look.

"All right. I will create. Don't know what or how, but there's a good five years of pent-up creative energy in here. Any ideas?"

At that moment, the waitress finally shows up with the chips and queso.

As if in response to his question, Christa turns to Klara. "Before we get to that, you absolutely have to tell me, lovely girl, what *mi ahijado* was like in high school."

Rosario returns to his slouch. "Oh, God . . ."

Klara laughs. "Don't slouch, Ros. You'll have a chance to tell your side of the story."

He has been third wheel to too many girl-hangs in his life to think he will actually get this chance. "Oh, really. And when will that be?"

"Hm. I mean, not that it's my business to tell you how to use your Diamond, but have you ever thought about writing a book?"

SOULBOUND

Friday nights, the Witch Queen and Soul Collector attend to the streets of the French Quarter. Residents know not to be out and about at the witching hour, for it is no secret what foul fruits of this odd romance they do harvest. But there are those who travel from afar and pay no heed to the warnings of the locals.

"Ah, that's what comes from too much jazz and liquor": so says an early-morning congregant on his walk to the communal worship. The deaths are deemed unfortunate accidents; perhaps they could not tolerate the strong Louisiana bourbon. The slippery steps cause their bodies to drown in the Mississippi. A freak accident fells a grand piano onto a tramp.

It is for a Mardi Gras celebration that newlyweds Rosario and Harriet make a vacation to New Orleans, something they each have long wished to do, but never would do alone. Now that they have each other, the world seems much smaller and everything seems much more attainable. Their first evening on holiday is filled with merry times and dancing, and they are the last two out of the club. Before heading home, they find a picturesque bench at Woldenberg Park, where they sit and talk well into the night. It is around three in the morning when they head back to the AirBnb, a comfortable house in the suburbs of Storyville.

The joyous day comes crashing down as they see ahead in the distance a grand piano collapse on an unsuspecting man. If they looked farther up at this moment, they would see the Witch Queen and Soul Collector cackling at their favorite trick in the book. They live for the sound it makes, a combination of notes and crashes reverberating in the night. But without looking up to see the assassins and avoid the same fate, the horrified Rosario and Harriet run to the wreckage to see if the man is all right.

As they approach, they see a green light emanating from the rubble. A mixture of gas and liquid, the light floats up into the air and, for a moment, performs a mesmerizing dance before being drawn upward. Looking up, Rosario and Harriet see the light drawn in by a strange-looking man holding a vial. He wears a dirty top hat and supports himself using a skull-topped cane, though his face is young. For a moment, he is illuminated by the green light approaching his vial, but upon its capture, he is hidden by shadow once more. Before their eyes can adjust, Rosario and Harriet hear a shrill woman's voice shouting.

"They have seen us; don't let them escape!"

The Witch Queen and Soul Collector leap down from the top of the building. They have the appearance of costumed demons, but Rosario and Harriet doubt they are mere costumes. Not interested in sticking around to figure out, they run as fast as they can away from the scene.

Seeing them run, the Witch Queen shrieks in frustration.

"Do not worry, my love," says the Soul Collector. "I had my eye on them already. The bats are on their way."

The Witch Queen shrieks again, but this time in delight.

"Wonderful, darling."

After several minutes of running, Rosario and Harriet find themselves on the west side of the French Quarter. When they realize the two strangers have not chased them, they take a chance to catch their breath.

"What. Was. That?"

"Harriet, do you believe in ghosts?"

"Oh my God, babe, you don't think?"

"What was that green light? Who were those two? I don't know and I don't care! We need to get out of this city right now."

"Rosario . . ."

"What?"

She points over his shoulder. Rosario turns around and sees around a hundred bats flying toward them, less than a football field away.

"What is happening!"

They continue running. After a minute or so, they pass another couple kissing in an alley. They try to warn them.

"Hello! Hey! *Run!*"

But the couple don't hear them until it is too late. Sensing a newer, easier prey, the bats cape down onto the kissing couple.

Looking back, Rosario sees the same green lights emerging from the feeding frenzy.

"Honestly, not a bad way to go."

After a few minutes of running, they arrive at their AirBnb. Harriet takes out the key and unlocks the door. Rosario immediately starts packing their things while Harriet calls an Uber to take them to the airport.

Five minutes later, the bags are packed and the Uber has arrived. But as they start to leave, they see a shiny green light outside the door.

"Oh my god, it's them."

"Quick, out the back!"

The green light is there too.

The Witch Queen is pacing outside, losing her patience. "Quit playing and kill them already!"

The Soul Collector is there, floating the house five feet off the ground.

"I'm getting to it!"

But before he has an opportunity to do anything, Rosario and Harriet run screaming out the front door. They look like savages wielding luggage bags like weapons. Unaware that the building they were in a second before is no longer attached to the earth, the two fall flat on their faces.

The humans stand up and look at each other, then at the two demon people. There is a moment of tension, then the Witch Queen furiously turns around and walks away. She lifts up her right hand over her head and snaps. "Come on, Laurent."

He hesitates. After a frustrated sigh, he drops the house. "Yes, dear."

From an inside coat pocket, he pulls out a vial, uncorks it, and points it at the two humans.

The bodies of Rosario and Harriet fall lifeless on the ground.

When Rosario wakes up again, he is sitting alone in a big room. It is a big library of some sort, top-to-bottom bookshelves on each wall. The chair is very nice red Corinthian leather, but dusty. He looks at his arms and hands. Everything seems normal, maybe a little desaturated. He rubs his eyes, but gently, so as to not mess up his contacts. This is when he realizes he is no longer wearing contacts.

"Hello?" he shouts.

Silence.

He looks down at his clothes. His Mardi Gras beads and club attire have been replaced by torn black rags. He reaches a hand up to his head. A goddam bowler hat on his head. Rosario takes a deep breath.

"*AAAAHHHHHHHH!*"

In the room next door, Harriet is already up and busy dusting the shelves. In the middle of the room, the two demon people are talking.

"And then maybe, after next week, we can go to Tomorrowland Dubai. Hundreds, thousands of souls! Most are on drugs; it'll be lovely!"

The Witch Queen scoffs. "Whatever. Have you checked on the ghosts?"

"Um, I've been with you the whole time, so . . ."

Harriet can almost feel the icy glare of annoyance the Witch Queen just gave. She hears the footsteps of the Soul Collector as he walks to the door.

It is then that they hear Rosario screaming in the next door.

The Witch Queen shrieks in delight. "Oh boy!"

The Soul Collector heads through the door, gently shuts it behind him.

The Witch Queen walks over to a table by where Harriet is dusting and pours herself something dark and red.

"Men, am I right?"

Harriet is confused. Is she talking to her? She stops dusting and turns to look at her.

The Witch Queen is undeniably beautiful. Her skin is pale and her hair is black, but her eyes have a thousand rainbow fires flickering within. Her clothes are a majestic, lacey burgundy and black with purple accents. Yet her demeanor is sad, tired, almost worried.

"Tell me about it," says Harriet. "At least your man is with you all the time. Rosario works on a cruise ship for two months at a time and then comes home for one."

"Oh no, never. Laurent stays right where I can see him. You stick around, you'll see. His eyes and thoughts are always wandering—it's sickening." Then she pauses. "Hold on. How are you guys able to make that work? How do you know if he's . . ."

the Witch Queen looks at the door her husband just went into . . . "staying faithful?"

"Well, I suppose there are two answers to that." At this point, Harriet, duster in hand, has made her way to join the Witch Queen on the other side of the table. "One, I trust him. He doesn't try to please me all the time, but he isn't insensitive to my feelings either. I love to support what he's doing and it's hard having him gone, but when he is here, he makes up for it by truly *being* here, you know what I mean?"

The Witch Queen sneers. "Cute. Human. Foolish. And your second answer is?"

"My second answer." Harriet tries not to show how offended she is. There are so many things floating through her head. At first, she thinks she'll give another serious answer. Then she realizes that the Witch Queen maybe isn't ready for that conversation. "My second answer is . . . it's not like he can do better! Not with that droopy left eye."

"Hah!" The Witch Queen does a spit-take. "I'm gonna like you! What was your earth name?"

"Harriet, Your Majesty. Harriet Davez."

"Wonderful. You shall be my new voodoo doll, Harriet Davez. Come with me. And—" she smiles—"call me Delphine."

With a flourish, the Witch Queen gets up and goes through the same door the Soul Collector went through five minutes earlier. Harriet gives herself a moment to remember she is terrified. Then she looks around at all the books. Best to make the most of this situation. She walks through the door, tossing the duster behind her as she goes.

"So, you see, that's how Delphine and I came to be living in this big mansion here in the underworld. It's very nice and we have lots of captured souls working for us as maids, butlers, cooks, et cetera. She's really the most wonderful, most beautiful Witch Queen you'll ever meet, though lately—" he pauses, looks towards the door, then decides not to get into it. "Anyways, would you prefer paperback or hardback?"

The Soul Collector, or Laurent, has just flipped a switch that opened up one of the walls to reveal a large and bizarre-looking glass mechanism. It inches forward on a revolving platform, and a whitish smoke comes out the back.

"Um, I guess I always preferred the luxury feel of a hardback," says Rosario. "How about you?"

Rosario is reminded of a time when he was a small, rambunctious boy of seven in second grade. It seemed at the time he was always in trouble, but he never knew why. All the adults in his life were, for one reason or another, almost perpetually disappointed in something he did. This confused him because he didn't feel he was doing anything that warranted such a reaction. Eventually, Rosario discovered things like common sense and social norms and reading body language, and he was grateful to have lived to the ripe old age of thirty without ever having to be confused again.

Now that he is dead, it is frustrating to find himself back again in that spiraling world of confusion.

"Yeah, I would agree with you," says Laurent. "Hardback really makes you feel like you're getting your money's worth. In fact . . ."

Rosario stares at the demon in front of him and tries to orient himself to everything he has been told in the last five minutes.

He and Harriet died about an hour ago.

Their souls were taken from their bodies and stored in vials for the journey to the Witch Queen and Soul Collector's mansion in the underworld.

Their souls were then placed into carbon copies of their original earth forms.

This whole underworld thing allegedly works something like a middle realm between the earth and the afterlife. The two demons haunt the streets of New Orleans at night, stealing souls from unsuspecting ravers and drunks.

At least it is not a hopeless case, Rosario thinks. *Isn't there a clause or something in the movie* Beetlejuice *that allows for souls to be brought back?*

Harriet has supposedly already awoken and is to be a servant in the mansion.

"It's actually very rare for a Soulbound to choose paperback . . ."

"I'm sorry to interrupt, Laurent. Just one question. You said Harriet is to be a servant in the mansion. Maybe I missed it: did you say what is going to happen to me as well?"

"Ah, well . . ."

Before the Soul Collector can answer, the Witch Queen bursts through the door, followed by Harriet.

"Laurent!"

"Babe!"

"Rosario!"

"Babe!"

Harriet runs to Rosario but before she can get very far, the Witch Queen summons her back. Harriet's body tenses up and is floated back next to the Queen.

"Laurent, why are you not done yet? I want to read this one *now*."

His shoulders rise as he's about to explain the long, tedious process, but he shrugs instead.

"Yes, darling."

Without stopping, the Witch Queen and Harriet pass through the room out another door.

"Uh," says Rosario.

"Yes? You were saying?" says Laurent.

Rosario is starting to feel that, in spite of the Soul Collector's politeness, this is really a bad situation he and Harriet are in. He also feels like Laurent's marriage could use a good spanking, though he can hardly consider himself an expert on underworld romances.

"Um, you were about to tell me what you were planning on doing with me."

"Ah, yes. You're going to become a book."

"He's going to become a *what?*"

"Yes, yes. He's going to become a book. And I anticipate a good one. You should have seen your shiny green souls within that vial. Yours just kind of floated around. Your man's? A

Tasmanian devil. I can't wait to see what kinds of crazy stuff happened in his life."

"Your highness,—*ahem*, Delphine." She pauses, trying to word this next question just right. "Wouldn't it be better if, I don't know, maybe you got him to actually tell you stories from his life? Rosario is a wonderful storyteller, very dramatic, very passionate. He recently wrote a book, actually. We have a copy with us!"

It occurs to her at that moment they probably didn't bring their luggage with them.

"Oh, Harriet, it's fine. The books always come out as if the Soulbounds themselves wrote them. Laurent does keep up with human books so maybe he has read it. Regardless, it'll be good for you to get away from him. You don't know how to really control your man. Which reminds me . . ."

Harriet and the Witch Queen are now in a sort of dungeon room filled with vials. Not like the one the Soul Collector captured them in, but rather larger and more ornate. The vials line the walls, and in the middle of the room is a smoldering cauldron.

"Sit."

Immediately Harriet is thrust into a chair while the Witch Queen sorts through her stores. She picks out three vials and brings them to the cauldron. Pouring in one, she chants.

"*Tripe of the swine make his desire only mine.*"

The cauldron bursts into blue flame. She pours in the next.

"*Eye of the Democrat for his love at first sight.*"

A smoky donkey floats out and dissipates in the air. And finally . . .

"Heart of a Christian, obedient and fun."

With this, the cauldron boils over. The Witch Queen takes an empty vial and fills it.

"Come."

Harriet is released from the chair and they make their way back through the door they went in. But before they leave, Harriet grabs a mirror from off the door and hides it behind her back.

"So, what is the potion for?" she asks.

"What, couldn't you tell? I'm going to put a spell on Laurent to make him mine forever. I'm tired of the way he looks at other girls." She stops and turns to Harriet. "The way he looks at you."

"Excuse me?"

"Yeah. It's just an unnecessary fault of his. So, I'm going to get rid of it. You gave me the idea, actually. When I saw how pathetic your relationship to your man was, I realized I couldn't let that happen with me and Laurent. Besides, my man isn't ugly like yours."

"Rosario isn't ugly!"

"You're the one who mentioned his eye droop. Now I can't look away. Ugh."

"Delphine! Um, I, I really don't think that's a good idea. If he loves you, a potion isn't going to make that better, and if he doesn't love you, a potion isn't going to change him."

"Oh, darling. You have a lot to learn about the underworld."

When they return to the book room, they find Rosario and the Soul Collector talking.

"... so that's why in the prequels, Jar Jar was *actually* the one orchestrating everything ..."

"Laurent!"

"Yes?"

What happens next happens quickly. The Witch Queen opens the vial, which shoots out a pink-and-blue liquid that lands square on the Soul Collector's face. She cackles maniacally as he wipes his face. Once he's wiped the liquid out of his eyes, he looks up to face his demonic bride.

But at that moment, Harriet yeets the mirror she's been hiding. It flies in between the Soul Collector and the Witch Queen so instead of seeing her, the first face the now-enchanted demon man sees is Rosario's.

The Soul Collector turns back to Rosario and admires him from afar, entranced with love. The Witch Queen is furious and stretches forth her hands to cast another spell on him. Before she is able to, Harriet has tipped over one of the bookshelves, sending a torrent of Soulbound books on top of her.

Whatever powers were holding Rosario to the chair have now broken, and he jumps out and grabs Harriet so they can escape.

Let the chase begin.

Door after door, the humans try to find a way out of the mansion while avoiding the demons who inhabit it.

"Like the day we met!" Rosario cries.

It is an ungodly maze. Sprinting through the rooms, they are glad to find that in the underworld, they can still move quickly. Faster, at least, than the Witch Queen and Soul Collector. Behind one door, they find a big kitchen where they can hide and catch their breath.

"Do you have any idea where we are?"

Harriet flashes an annoyed look. "What do you think?"

"You walked around with the queen bitch; what did you see?"

"Nothing! I mean, there was a library, then there was the book room that you were in, and a dungeon."

"You didn't see a window or anything?"

"No, there wasn't."

She stops.

"Wait, there was a small window in the dungeon. We might be too big, but if we can get there, it might be our best chance."

At that moment, they hear a crashing of pots and pans. It is the Soul Collector.

"Rosario, sweetie, I know you're in here!"

"Don't move a muscle," whispers Harriet.

They are crammed underneath the sink, him little spoon, her big. He picks up a dirty frying pan to attack, but in doing so he makes a slight *clink*.

"There you are!"

The sound of feet approaching them.

"Now!" Rosario shouts.

Harriet uses her legs to launch the full weight of her man at the legs of the Soul Collector, who falls over. Rosario hits him over the head with the pan.

"We're like the Looney Tunes up in here."

"Run!"

The two get the hell out of Dodge. Harriet is confident that if they can find any of the first rooms, she can get to the dungeon and out the window—but first they have to avoid the Witch Queen.

In her makeshift throne room, the Witch Queen has gathered her top servants to hand out instructions.

"You have one mission. Find the humans and bring them to me."

"Um, Your Majesty, where is your husband?"

"Oh, yeah. Find him too."

"Yes, Your Majesty."

A moment passes.

"Well? Don't just stand there!"

The servants of the mansion disperse like the Marx Brothers. One trips over a couch, another steps on a rake and slams herself in the face, still another tries to pull open a push door and it takes just a second too long to realize his mistake.

The Witch Queen sinks back into her throne and sighs. Surrounded by idiots.

There was a time when things were different with Laurent. Lately, it seems to her like he is just collecting souls because he is afraid. Of what? She doesn't know. Maybe he is afraid it's the only way to get her to like him. But that's ridiculous! She loves him more than anyone else in the whole world.

Once she can use the spell on him properly, it will all work out. They can go back to haunting the streets of New Orleans and making love whenever she is in the mood.

After running through what seems like an eternity of rooms and dodging a dozen or more servants, Rosario and Harriet eventually make it back to the library. They are about to go into the book room to get down into the dungeon when they peek through a crack in the door and see there are four servants cleaning up the mess from the start of the chase.

"I think if we're quiet, we can walk along the wall behind them and get to the door to the dungeon."

"Rosario, for the love of God. *Please* try to be quiet."

They gently open the door and begin their tiptoe.

Almost there.

So close to redemption.

"Hey! You two! Why aren't you helping us?"

They freeze.

"Wait a minute, who are you? I haven't seen you before."

Rosario gets an idea.

"Oh, us?"

Harriet holds back a swear word.

"Yeah, we're new. My name is Brad and this is my wife Angelina. We're looking for the two humans who escaped. Witch Queen wants us to check the dungeon."

"Ah, okay, got it. Well, if you find them, they've got a lot of cleaning up here to do!"

"Will do. What's your name by the way?"

"Henry Ford."

"Great to meet you, Mr. Ford."

They open the door to the dungeon and head inside.

The Witch Queen is pacing through the mansion, not wanting to work up a sweat. She loves walking through her palace and yelling at the servants; it always cheers her up.

When she gets to the kitchen and sees her husband lying on the floor with a big purple bruise on his head, she feels a twinge of remorse. She goes to him and rests his head on her lap. She recites a spell to heal the bruise and wakes him up. There is a rare sweetness in her eyes.

"How are you feeling, Laurent?"

He struggles to open his eyes. When he does, he immediately scrunches his face; the light is too strong. After a minute or so, he looks up at her with the most sober face she's ever seen on him. "Please, honey. Let me go." It takes him more energy than he reasonably has to spare at the moment.

The Witch Queen is shocked. Whom does he think he is talking to?

"Darling, please. All the spells, all the magic. Just let me go. My heart can't handle it anymore."

She looks down at his big brown eyes.

She sees immense pain.

It occurs to her the pain has been there for a long time.

"Sugar, what are you talking about?"

"It used to be so fun, Delphine. Haunting the streets of New Orleans with you, coming back here and partying with all the neighbors, knowing that your magic was keeping us from ever truly dying. But now you've become this obsessive control monster, and I just can't take it. No one wants to hang out with us anymore because they're afraid you're going to enslave them or turn them into books. I miss people. This isn't an existence I want anymore, Delphine. Please, darling . . ."

He gulps. "Just let me die."

Delphine thinks back to what Harriet told her. Has she truly become an obsessive control monster? The thought breaks her heart. She begins to cry. She looks down again at her husband.

The tears are in his eyes, too.

With a slow twist of her hand, she draws the spell out of him. Then she draws out all the other spells she has placed on him over the years. When she is done, a frail old man lies there in her arms.

"Thank you."

She helps him up and watches as he exits the kitchen. He does not look back.

In the top corner of the dungeon sits a lone window, big enough for at least Harriet. They barricade the door.

"I'll fit through the window, no problem," she says. "Help me up and then I'll yank you out."

"I love when you yank me out."

It is a tight squeeze, but Harriet eventually is through. The cool night air is refreshing on her skin. She bends down to reach for him.

"This is going to hurt, but we're gonna get you out!"

She begins yanking on his right arm. Rosario realizes before Harriet that it just isn't going to work.

"Ow! Ow! Harriet! Stop, please!"

But she keeps tugging at his arm.

"I! Won't! Let! You! Become! A! Book!"

"Harriet!"

There is a rare depth in his voice. She looks down at Rosario's head, at his arm she is tugging at. They have cracked the edge of the windowpane, and blood is dripping from his left shoulder.

He motions for her to sit down. She sits.

"You know, when Laurent told me he was going to turn me into a book, you know what I immediately thought of? I thought of you, and I thought of that book of short stories I wrote when I turned thirty. You remember that? We were still new to each other, so there was only one story that had you in it. I called it 'The Auctioneer's Daughter.' You remember that? I thought about my life before you and my life with you. They are such different existences!" He starts choking up. "I just love you so much!"

She starts choking up.

"My godmother once told me that my duty as a Diamond host was to create and create and create, because we live in an art-killing world, but I will succeed at everything as long as I find my genuine expression. And you know what, babe? That genuine expression is you! Harriet! Loving you fulfills me like nothing ever has in my life. I have loved spending these last few years with you. Learning you, learning about you, learning about what love truly means with you. I see God's love in you. I am ready to face whatever is coming my way. Now go, get out of here and live a beautiful life with—"

CRASH.

Rosario stops. The window he was just trapped in has shattered around him, and the bricks of the mansion have blown up, creating a massive hole in the wall. He feels his body being taken out of the hole, back inside the dungeon. He floats onto the floor. Looking up, he sees the Witch Queen. She has Harriet in a tight hold and floats her back inside as well.

She releases her.

Harriet goes to Rosario and starts to mop up his brow.

"Out of the way, voodoo doll."

But this time, she doesn't force Harriet to move. They look at each other, then Harriet stands up. Delphine lifts her hand toward Rosario. A gentle blue mist disperses over his shoulder and heals the wound from the windowpane. The two humans look at each other and then at the Witch Queen, in shock.

"You two are free to go."

They don't move, initially. But, not willing to see her change her mind, Harriet helps Rosario up and they walk out of the dungeon and into the book room. Looking back, they see the Witch Queen lowering her head to cry.

They pass the servants, still picking up the books in the book room.

"See ya 'round, Henry Ford."

The door that leads out of the book room now opens up to a big hallway, at the end of which appears the front door.

They pass the kitchen where Rosario KO'd the Soul Collector.

Before they reach the front door, they see the dead body of a frail old man. Next to the corpse, they see a vial with a lively green soul jumping around inside. Harriet picks it up and sees attached to the vial is a note that says:

"My soul is yours."

She holds nothings back.

"DELPHINE!"

It's so loud Rosario throws himself on the ground.

"DELPHINE! YOUR LOVER!"

The Witch Queen comes out and Harriet gives her the vial. She reads it, then opens the cap and drinks the contents. After a few seconds, she lets out a bright purple flame that engulfs the old man's corpse. It is so bright, the humans have to shield their eyes.

When they look again, the old man who had been lying on the ground not two seconds earlier has turned into the young, vibrant Soul Collector once more.

The demons embrace and make out. Rosario starts humming Berlin's "Take My Breath Away."

Delphine is laugh-crying. "Laurent! Why did you come back?"

"Because I love you, baby. I always have, always will. You don't need to control me or put spells on me. All that does is limit the ways I can love you."

Delphine flashes a knowing grin at Harriet.

"You know your stuff, voodoo doll."

Turning to the humans, the Soul Collector says, "Feel free to come visit whenever you want. I know we haven't given you the nicest welcome, but now that you've helped our marriage, know that this mansion will once again be home to the greatest parties this side of existence. Next time you come to New Orleans, just be out and about for the Witching Hour and you'll find us. We do love to party. Also, don't worry about your bodies. Our bats have completely disintegrated them, so you can keep the ones you have now. Sorry about the clothes and your luggage though."

Harriet is about to ask a fury of questions, but Delphine interrupts.

"Once you go out these doors you'll be back in New Orleans, outside your Airbnb. Is there anything else you need?"

Without missing a beat, Rosario says, "Six million dollars."

"Okay."

Out of thin air, Delphine creates a suitcase with a big money sign on it and gives it to him.

The demons kiss again.

Laurent is alive with a new energy. Not taking his eyes off Delphine, he says, "Now, what do you say we let these humans go back to their world so you and I can get a little *Nutcracker* in?"

The humans look surprised. The demons turn around and walk back toward the book room hand-in-hand, looking like newlyweds.

"Wait a minute. Bro, did you read my book of short stories?"

Laurent laughs. "Maybe a little bit."

ABOUT THE AUTHOR
AND ILLUSTRATOR

Orlando Diaz saw the Mary Poppins movie when he was a kid and was inspired by the character Bert to be anything he ever wanted, so he studied classical piano at the Eastman School of Music and then worked as a sushi chef, US Army bandperson, landscaper, real estate investor, musical theater director, financial advisor, piano bar entertainer, and deli clerk, along with other fun jams. This is his first book.

Orlando can be reached through his website,
www.orlandodiazpiano.com.

The great-grandson of Vaudevillians of yore, **Drew Cochran** is an author, illustrator, and game designer of *The Epic of Dreams RPG*. Meandering through different mediums of art and story, from visual illustration to mythic narrative to theatrical role play, he works to breathe ancient wonder back into a starving modern world. "Everything's a Christophany if you stare long enough."